COLD

JUSTICE

(A Carly Phoenix Mystery –Book 1)

Taylor Stark

Taylor Stark

Taylor Stark is author of the MARY CAGE mystery series, comprising five books (and counting); of the CARLY PHOENIX mystery series, comprising five books (and counting); and of the new SIENNA DUSK mystery series, comprising five books (and counting).

An avid reader and lifelong fan of the mystery and thriller genres, Taylor loves to hear from you, so please feel free to visit taylorstarkauthor.com to learn more and stay in touch.

ISBN: 978-1-0943-9874-7

BOOKS BY TAYLOR STARK

MARY CAGE SUSPENSE THRILLER
FAR FROM HERE (Book #1)
FAR FROM HOPE (Book #2)
FAR FROM SAFE (Book #3)
FAR FROM SIGHT (Book #4)
FAR FROM REACH (Book #5)

CARLY PHOENIX SUSPENSE THRILLER
COLD JUSTICE (Book #1)
COLD BLOODED (Book #2)
COLD TRUTH (Book #3)
COLD PURSUIT (Book #4)
COLD VENGEANCE (Book #5)

SIENNA DUSK SUSPENSE THRILLER
BENEATH THE FROST (Book #1)
BENEATH THE SURFACE (Book #2)
BENEATH THE LIES (Book #3)
BENEATH THE SILENCE (Book #4)
BENEATH THE WHISPERS (Book #5)

PROLOGUE

39 Years ago

Chicago's air was a frozen noose, wreathing the city in a bleak shroud. The merciless winter of 1985 had flung its icy mantle over every steel beam and cobblestone, turning the bustling metropolis into a painting of frosted stillness. Streetlights fought a losing battle against the encroaching dusk, their glow barely piercing the thickening veil of snowflakes that danced like ash from an unseen fire.

Emily Rosario exhaled a cloud of crystalline vapor as she pushed through the glass door of the diner, the bell above chiming a melancholy farewell. Her shift was done, the clatter of dishes and sizzle of the griddle yielding to the contemplative quiet of the evening. She tugged her coat tighter around her petite frame, the woolen fabric a paltry shield against the biting cold. A constellation of snowflakes clung to her dark curls, each one as unique as the myriad sketches that crowded her artist's portfolio. She was young and full of artistic grit.

Though slight in stature, Emily moved with the purposeful grace of a dancer, her steps leaving fleeting impressions in the freshly fallen snow. Her eyes, a deep brown reflecting a soul both dreamlike and vibrant, scanned the desolate streets with a painter's appreciation for contrast—the stark white of winter against the charcoal skeletons of leafless trees. If only she could paint the surrounding streets, capturing them in their frozen pose.

She felt the world around her with an intensity that fueled her creativity, her mind already reaching for the charcoal stick and paper that would transform the scene into art. But there was a sharp edge to the beauty tonight, a chilling foreboding that caused a tremor to run through her fingers—not from the cold, but from a sense of something else, something lurking just beyond perception.

As night claimed dominion over the sky, the streetlights cast elongated shadows that distorted reality, turning innocuous shapes into silent sentinels, watching Emily's solitary journey. Every crunch of her boots on the icy pavement was a staccato note in the eerie quiet of the winter evening. She was alone, yet the prickling at the back of her neck whispered of unseen eyes tracking her every move, like a predator sizing up its prey.

But Emily was no stranger to the city's mercurial moods; she embraced them, drawing inspiration from the struggle between light and darkness. Each step was an affirmation of her place in this urban labyrinth, her pulse a steady drumbeat defying the ominous atmosphere that sought to claim her spirit. She was alive, vibrant, and her soul ached with the pains and joys of the art world.

The snow continued to fall, a relentless cascade of white that seemed intent on burying the city, and with it, any trace of Emily Rosario's footsteps. Each light footstep made an impression, which slowly faded into the white burial shroud of snow.

Emily's breath formed swirling plumes that mingled with the frigid air as she made her way down the deserted avenue. The snow crunched beneath her weight, the only sound in the otherwise hushed world. She wore a heavy coat over her slight frame, the collar pulled high to ward off the biting chill. She moved with purpose, her dark eyes alert and scanning the surroundings—a canvas of white punctuated by the frigid silhouettes of barren trees on the sidewalks and vacant drivers moving off to unknown destinations.

Leaving the diner's warmth far behind, Emily felt the cold seeping through her layers, numbing her fingers despite the gloves clutched tightly around the strap of her satchel—her makeshift shield against the elements. Her art supplies jostled within, the charcoals and sketch pads she treasured, tools for capturing the city's essence in her work. She navigated the icy terrain with an artist's precision, each step carefully placed to avoid the treacherous patches where the ice lay thickest.

The streetlights flickered overhead, casting erratic shadows that danced across the snow, creating a mosaic of light and black. Emily's imagination swirled with the wind, envisioning spectral figures within these patterns, fleeting muses that spurred her creative heart even as a shiver ran through her bones.

A sudden rumble shattered the silence, and a truck edged into view. Its headlights cut through the falling snow like beacons, illuminating the path ahead. It rolled to a stop beside her, the driver's side window descending with a whir of mechanics. Inside, a young man leaned toward her, his features obscured by the dimness within the cab.

"Hey there! Need a lift?" he called out, his voice barely rising above the hum of the engine. "This weather is pretty bad, and it's only going to get worse."

He seemed close to her age, with a face that could belong to many of the locals she passed on her daily routine, yet there was nothing immediately recognizable about him.

Emily paused, assessing the situation. Shadows bathed the truck interior, but she could make out the outline of a worn leather jacket, the kind that had seen years of service against Chicago winters. His tone conveyed a casual concern, typical Midwestern politeness tinged with an undercurrent of something she couldn't quite place—a hint of eagerness, perhaps, or was it just her own apprehension coloring the interaction?

The snowfall intensified, a curtain of white that seemed to swallow the distance between her and the sanctuary of her apartment. On a clear day, the walk would have been invigorating, but now, each step forward promised only more cold, more isolation. She considered the offer, the truck's warm interior promising a brief reprieve from the winter's grasp.

Emily's breath formed puffs of mist that danced away into the night as she weighed her options. The snow underfoot squeaked in protest with every uncertain shift of her weight, a natural consequence of the bitter cold. She glanced once more at the truck, its engine a low purr against the hush of falling snow. Chicago's winter was unforgiving, and tonight it seemed to conspire to push her towards a decision she might not have made otherwise.

"Sure," Emily said, at last, the word more surrender than acceptance.

She approached the passenger side, her hand trembling slightly—whether from the cold or a latent sense of anxiety, she couldn't tell. Frost covered the door handle. She touched it, but it resisted her grip before yielding to the pressure of her fingers.

As Emily climbed into the truck, the dome light flicked on, casting an immediate glow that chased away the shadows. She glimpsed the man's hands as he shifted to give her space, and something primal within her tensed. They were large, disproportionate almost, with knuckles that seemed swollen from years of hard labor or perhaps from other less savory activities. He had trimmed nails, but they bore the dark crescents of grime beneath them, and there was a jagged scar running down the side of his thumb, white and worn against the weathered skin.

For a moment, those hands hovered in the air between them, as if they were entities unto themselves—capable of things beyond mere steering and shifting. Then, just as quickly, they retreated to the wheel, where one thumb tapped an irregular rhythm, a silent beat that filled the cab with an unnerving sort of anticipation.

He smiled. "Here we go."

Emily buckled herself in, folding her arms tightly across her chest, as if the gesture could somehow shield her from whatever uncertainties lay ahead. She stole another glance at the man's hands, watching how the tendons moved like taut wires beneath the surface of his skin, how they gripped the steering wheel with an assurance that belied the casual slouch of his posture.

"Thanks for this," she murmured, trying to sound more confident than she felt. "The weather's just terrible."

"Least I could do," he replied, his voice smooth, yet there was a rasp beneath it—a rough edge that spoke of cigarettes or whiskey, or long nights spent away from the comfort of home.

He put the truck into gear, and they pulled away from the curb, leaving behind the relative safety of the diner's neon sign for the uncertainty that lay enshrouded in the snow-filled streets of Chicago.

The horizon was a palette of gray, the sky indistinguishable from Lake Michigan's waters, which lay frozen and still. Here, Emily Rosario could feel the desolation of the place seeping into her bones. She had always thought of winter as a canvas awaiting the bold strokes of vibrant life she was so eager to create, but now it seemed like a different world altogether—void of color, void of warmth.

A gust of wind whipped at her cheeks, already chapped by the cold, and she turned her face away from the window, trying to focus on the interior of the truck. The scent of worn leather and motor oil wrapped around her, offering no real comfort. Her eyes roamed the dashboard's assortment of faded stickers and a dangling air freshener that had long since given up its scent. There was an intimacy in the clutter, a sense of someone's life lived within these metal walls, and it made her stomach tight with an unnameable anxiety.

Outside, the snowflakes began their descent in earnest, each one a silent thief coming to steal away the contours of the world she knew. They fell with purpose, relentless, a thickening veil that blurred the line between land and water, between safety and the unknown.

Emily watched as they gathered on the windshield, each flake joining another, until the glass became a shroud of white. The wipers struggled against the onslaught, leaving streaks that only momentarily cleared her view of the shoreline. With each swipe, the lake disappeared and reemerged, a mirage that played hide and seek with her senses.

Emily felt time slow down for a moment. As though something in the bleakness was speaking to her, warning to her. If only she had listened.

The world outside dwindled to a narrow tunnel of visibility, the edges softening until only the immediate space around the truck, an island adrift in a sea of white. The lights from other vehicles were distant stars, fading fast, and for a moment, Emily felt utterly alone with this stranger, moving through an expanse of cold indistinction.

He grinned, nodding to her. Emily saw something in his eyes, a glimmer of a man capable of terrible things. The truck drove on into the snow as quiet consumed the cabin.

No one ever saw or heard from Emily Rosario again.

CHAPTER ONE

39 years later

The concrete was a blur beneath Carly Phoenix's pounding feet, her breaths coming in sharp, controlled bursts. Her blonde hair blew in the stiff wind, ruffled as she did her best to keep up. The city's cacophony faded into the background as she zeroed in on the fleeing figure ahead—Jason Willard, the known brutal serial killer whose capture would mean safety for countless others.

Cary had been waiting for this moment. She could almost taste it.

Jason weaved through the streets, first traffic, then crowds of people, peering behind occasionally with dark, piercing eyes. Carly was worried that he would try to take as many people down with him as he could, but she knew she had to focus on putting him behind bars. Little else mattered.

Her focus narrowed to the rhythm of the chase; Jason Willard's coat flapping like a dark flag of defiance, taunting her as she rushed into the dangerous game of cat and mouse through the dense urban jungle.

Carly darted around pedestrians who became unwitting obstacles in the deadly pursuit. Horns blared as she bolted across traffic-choked streets, her mind tuning into the suspect's patterns. She expected his next move—a desperate veer into an alleyway choked with dumpsters and litter. Without hesitation, Carly followed, the gap closing between them, the grimy walls funneling them toward confrontation. She readied herself for a deadly showdown.

The alley ended abruptly, a chain-link fence looming ahead. The killer scaled it with a desperation no doubt born from the primal fear of captivity. Carly reached the barrier, hand over hand, her muscles screaming, but her determination louder. At the top, the killer kicked back, aiming to send her tumbling. Carly dodged, teeth gritted, losing no ground. Even though Jason Willard was now on the other side, moving away from her, she did not give up. She swung her legs over, boots hitting the ground with a jarring thud on the other side as the man stumbled onto the pavement ahead.

"Jason, FBI! Stop, or I'll shoot!" Carly's command sliced through the air, authoritative, demanding obedience. But the killer didn't look back. Carly's adrenaline spiked as she squeezed the trigger.

With a sharp crack, the bullet sliced through the frigid air, hitting the curb inches from Willard's feet. Chunks of concrete exploded into the icy night, sending fragments scattering like shrapnel. The sound reverberated off the desolate buildings around them, adding an eerie echo to the tense standoff. Willard froze, his eyes widening in shock as realization dawned that Carly was not one to be trifled with. The streetlights flickered overhead, casting long shadows that danced menacingly across the frozen ground, emphasizing the gravity of the moment.

As if seeing the indecision in Carly's eyes, he sped off once more towards a few buildings, half completed like a row of broken teeth.

They reached a construction site, rebar and concrete pillars the skeleton of some future edifice. The killer scrambled up a mound of debris, Carly right behind, her athleticism merging with raw instincts. He swiped at a stack of pipes, sending them rolling down towards her. She dodged, one slamming against her shoulder, pain radiating sharply. No time to acknowledge it.

"Enough!" she shouted, the word echoing off the steel bones around them.

"You'll have to kill me!" Jason screamed as he darted up a set of stairs.

Up and up they went, floor after floor.

At the pinnacle of the towering building, a precarious standoff unfolded between them, the sprawling city below indifferent to their impending struggle for survival. The killer, desperation blazing in his eyes, stood at a critical crossroads with limited options. Carly, her gaze chillingly clear, watched his ominous contemplation as he weighed the grim choice between a fatal fall and facing justice head-on. Determined not to let him dictate the outcome, she steeled herself for the perilous dance that awaited.

"You have no other options," Jason's voice cut through the tense air like a knife. "You know what you have to do, Carly. Pull the trigger." His words hung heavily in the room as Carly weighed her choices.

Despite the rational voice inside her urging caution and waiting for backup, Carly defiantly disregarded it and ventured onto the treacherous exterior of the building.

With a deafening crash, Jason and Carly collided in a harrowing struggle. Their bodies tangled and thrashed as they fought for dominance, grunting and gasping with each move. The outside was a blur of flailing limbs and pounding hearts, the air thick with the scent of sweat and fear. Fueled by adrenaline and anger, their battle escalated into a frenzied fight, each strike more fierce than the last. Jason's grip tightened around Carly's arm as he violently dragged her towards the edge, his eyes burning with fury.

"I'll take you with me!" he screamed.

She struggled against him, desperate to break free, but he was too strong. With one last shove, they both tumbled over the edge and descended into the darkness below.

Catching onto a railing with a thud, Jason pulled at her legs dangling below.

"There's no way but down! To death!" he cried, the night quietening around him.

Carly could feel her grip weakening with the weight of Jason on her. For a moment, she thought about kicking him off to save herself. But she knew, killer or not, she wouldn't be able to live with that. Then she saw it, a piece of scaffolding jutting out next to her dangling legs.

With unwavering determination etched on her face, Carly deftly secured the cold metal handcuffs around Jason's wrists, binding him tightly to the corroded scaffold.

"No!" He cried. "You can't!"

"Too late," she said, panting breathlessly. "You'll see the inside of a courtroom if it kills me."

Now, resignation finally swept across Jason Willard's face as he dangled from the metal structure.

As Carly found herself suspended above a gaping chasm, the abyss yawning beneath her feet, a chilling sense of vertigo gripped her. The void below beckoned with a sinister allure, its darkness whispering promises of oblivion.

Her fingers strained against the weight of her own body as she clung to the unforgiving scaffold, each second ticking by like an eternity. The rusty metal groaned under the strain, echoing in the desolate space around them. Beads of sweat gathered on Carly's forehead, mingling with the icy chill of fear that coursed through her veins. She teetered on the edge of a precipice, both physical and metaphorical; her resolve tested to its very limits.

In a heart-stopping moment that seemed to stretch into infinity, Carly battled against the relentless pull of gravity threatening to claim her.

"Agent Phoenix!" a voice then shouted from above.

Just when all seemed lost and fate dangled precariously over uncertainty's edge, several shadowy figures materialized on the scene—backup officers, emerging like guardian angels from the night above.

"Are you okay?" one officer shouted down.

"No!" Carly yelled. "I'm about to be a stain on the sidewalk if you guys don't get down here, fast!"

The officers climbed out, nervous towards her, and that was when Carly felt fear the most.

*

Carly's breaths came out in controlled bursts as she navigated the sterile corridors of the FBI headquarters, her boots silent on the polished floor. The air was thick with the scent of wax and latent ambition. She knew acutely that every agent she passed had heard about her latest collaring — they eyed her with a mix of admiration and caution, like she was some feral creature that had wandered into civilization.

She paused before the frosted glass door emblazoned with Director Lewis Hargrove's name, straightened her jacket, and knocked sharply. At the gruff "Enter" from within, she pushed open the door.

The office was a study in austere efficiency: every book spine perfectly aligned, each award glistening under the lights, the American flag standing sentinel in the corner. Hargrove sat behind his massive oak desk, the lines on his face etched deeper by years of service and skepticism.

"Agent Phoenix," he said without preamble, his voice laced with an edge that didn't bode well.

"Sir," Carly replied, maintaining a neutral tone despite the thrumming anticipation of a reprimand.

"Sit," Hargrove ordered, gesturing to the chair opposite him. It might as well have been a defendant's seat in a courtroom. She complied, back straight, eyes locked on his.

"Your stunt today." Hargrove's words were clipped and precise. "Reckless doesn't cover it."

Carly opened her mouth, but a look from Hargrove silenced her. This wasn't a debate; it was a sentencing.

"Your record is impressive, Phoenix," he continued. "Smart, quick, intuitive—but what you pulled today? That's not how we operate. Not only did you put yourself in danger, but you risked the life of the suspect in your care, not to mention the public."

He let the words hang in the air for a moment, heavy with disappointment. Carly felt them like a punch to the gut, but she kept her expression impassive.

"Director Hargrove, I..." But she didn't have time to defend herself.

He waved his hand. "The Bureau doesn't need another high-profile stain on its reputation. First Jack Fritz going AWOL and ending up in an institute, and then agent Martens caught getting kickbacks from the mob. We'd quite like it if the FBI could have a positive story in the press for once."

Hargrove threw a newspaper down on the table between them. There was a still from a security camera on the front, revealing Carly brandishing a gun in a crowded street. The headline wasn't much better.

"It's not how it looks," Carly said. "I've worked damned hard for the agency, and I got Willard, didn't I? No one got hurt."

"But they could have," Hargrove said, softening his tone.

"So that's it then, I'm gone?" Carly said with frustration. "Five years on the Bureau wiped out because I did my job?"

"You're not being fired," Hargrove said.

Carly felt confused. "Then what?"

"Effective immediately, you're being reassigned," Hargrove declared, his gaze unwavering. "You're off the Behavioral Analysis Unit to keep you away from high-profile killers. I'm transferring you to Cold Cases."

The words hit Carly with the force of a physical blow. From the adrenaline-fueled hunt of active predators to the silent company of regret and unanswered questions. It was a clear demotion, a signal to rein in her fiery methods.

"Where?"

"Out of harm's way for the moment. Chicago field office," Hargrove added, sealing her fate. He slid a manila folder across the desk towards her, its contents her new reality.

This made it worse. Carly had grown up in Chicago, and after a tough childhood there, had done everything she could to avoid ever going back.

She wanted to fight. But for now, she'd left her tank empty from the fight with Willard the day before. Even if she could have, she knew the decision would not be reversed any time soon.

"Understood, sir," Carly said, her voice steady despite the storm of protest raging inside her. She took the folder, the papers within representing the sharp turn her career had just taken.

"Dismissed," Hargrove finished, already turning his attention to the paperwork on his desk, a clear sign that the conversation — and perhaps Carly's time in the spotlight — was over.

Carly nodded and stood up.

"Listen to me, Carly." Hargrove's use of her first name felt like a warning shot. "You are one of the best agents this Bureau has seen in a long time, but that doesn't give you carte blanche. If you keep up this cowboy behavior, you won't last much longer in the FBI. Not under my or anyone else's watch. You have to learn to rein yourself in."

The finality in his tone brooked no argument, and Carly felt the fight drain out of her. She stood perfectly still, absorbing the blow. His gaze held hers, unyielding and resolute, and in it, she saw the gulf between their definitions of duty.

"Is that understood?" Hargrove asked, his voice a low rumble in the deepening quiet of the office.

"Understood," Carly replied, her response automatic, but her glare remained fixed on Hargrove, hard as flint. She turned on her heel, leaving the confrontation hanging unfinished in the air behind her.

Outside Hargrove's office, the hallways of the Bureau stretched out before her, filled with agents who played by the rules, their paths clear and unobstructed. Carly's path had never been so straightforward, and as she walked, her mind raced, plotting her next move within the confines of her new boundaries. The chase was on hold, but the hunt was far from over.

Carly moved across the polished floors of the FBI office, a percussive echo in the ticking clockwork of her mind. She strode past cubicles and closed doors, her sharp gaze never wavering, even as her career path veered into unexpected territory.

"Phoenix," a voice called from behind, but Carly didn't falter, didn't turn. She knew who it was; she knew what they wanted. Sympathy, shock, maybe even gossip—none of which interested her. She was being reassigned and demoted, and there was nothing left to say.

The elevator dinged its arrival, and Carly stepped inside, pressing the button for the parking garage with more force than necessary. The doors slid shut, encapsulating her in a steel box that mirrored the confinement she felt. Yet, within that space, there was clarity. This was not an end, but a beginning. Her methods might be unorthodox, but they were effective. And she would prove it, regardless of the title under her badge or the city skyline outside her window.

As the elevator descended, Carly's thoughts shifted, zeroing in on Chicago. The word tasted like history, bitter and unresolved. It was where she'd grown up, where she'd vowed never to return—a place fraught with personal demons. But now, whether she liked it, it was her future.

She knew she would have to face those demons once and for all.

CHAPTER TWO

The skyline emerged like a bristling spine of steel and glass, a familiar beast in the distance that grew more imposing as Carly Phoenix's rental car ate up the miles on I-90. Chicago, with its relentless energy and towering monuments to human ambition, was both a graveyard of her past and now an arena for redemption.

As she exited the expressway, the city streets welcomed her with their intermittent chorus of honks and sirens—a soundtrack she hadn't realized she'd missed until this moment. The neighborhoods blurred past, each one a patchwork quilt of memories, frayed and faded with time.

Carly's eyes, usually so keen and penetrating when dissecting a suspect or crime scene, softened as they traced the lines of the city. She passed the old neon cinema where she'd had her first kiss; it was a pharmacy now, cold and sterile. The park where she scraped her knees learning to ride a bike remained, though the trees seemed taller, their branches more gnarled and wise.

Then there was her old family home. The house looked well taken care of, more than it had been when she was a child. She could almost hear her mother shouting at her to come in off the street and have something to eat. That thought made her shudder. She had to move on.

The streets were arteries, pumping Carly through the heart of her history, veins that held stories of scraped knees and youthful revelries. Each corner turned was another page of her life, dog-eared and dusty from disuse, but indelibly inked into her being. The city was a paradox, a sanctuary of memories and a crucible for the living, and Carly felt the weight of both as she drove.

She passed by the high school she once attended, its brick facade unchanged, yet everything around it transformed. Old hangout spots had given way to trendy cafes and boutiques, making her feel like an interloper in her own past. The familiarity was there, but it was distant, like a melody you can hum but can't remember the words to.

Every streetlight cast long shadows that seemed to whisper of the girl Carly used to be, before the FBI, before the chase that went south, before her recklessness cost her the BAU position she prized. Those shadows beckoned, tempting her to dwell in the what-ifs and might-have-beens, but Carly knew better than to succumb to them.

She was here on a mission, after all, even if it wasn't the one she wanted. Demoted and reassigned, yes, but not defeated. Carly was someone who thrived under pressure, who sharpened her resolve on the whetstone of adversity.

The car's tires hummed a steady rhythm against the asphalt as she navigated the grid, a lullaby of motion that lulled her deeper into reflection. Buildings streamed by, each holding fragments of her former self, pieces she would pick up and examine in the quiet moments between cases. But for now, she pushed those thoughts aside, focusing on the road ahead and the cold cases that awaited her—puzzles that time had obscured, waiting for a mind like hers to piece them back together.

As Carly pulled up to the curb of her new, albeit temporary, place to live, the last rays of the setting sun dipped below the horizon, painting the sky in hues of bruising purples and oranges. Night was falling over Chicago, the city that shaped her, and Carly wondered how long she would be within its embrace.

*

Carly's fingers curled around the set of keys the landlord had just passed to her, a diminutive man who reminded her of a murderous accountant she once put in prison. The key's cold metal pushed against the warmth still lingering in her palms from the firm handshake. She glanced up at the apartment building, its brick facade neither new nor crumbling—an intermediate state that echoed her current standing with the FBI. The door to the lobby creaked on old hinges as she stepped inside, the sound slicing through the quiet like an uneasy whisper.

The apartment was on the third floor, accessible via a staircase that had known better days. Each step seemed to groan under the weight of her footsteps, the echo trailing behind her like a hesitant shadow. Inside, the space was modest: hardwood flooring, white walls in need of a fresh coat of paint, and windows that looked out onto the bustling streets of Chicago.

"Temporary," Carly murmured to herself, setting her duffel bag down with a soft thud. This wasn't her home—not really. It was merely a staging ground, a place to regroup until she could claw her way back into the Behavioral Analysis Unit and get her career back on track.

She paced the sparse living room; her strides purposeful, each footfall a silent proclamation of intent. The apartment would do, for now, a tactical retreat rather than a surrender. But as the evening light faded and gave way to the artificial glow of street lamps, a knot of frustration tightened in her gut.

She thought of her mother, dead. Her father... Then there was Justin, her brother. Carly had looked after him when she was barely an adult, and he still a kid. Now, they hadn't spoken for some time, and the guilt of that had plagued Carly.

Carly sank into a creaky chair by the window, the fabric rough beneath her touch, the springs yielding reluctantly to her weight. Her gaze traveled across the rooftops and through the tangle of alleyways below, where shadows danced just beyond the reach of light. Displacement gnawed at her, a sense of being uprooted from the life she knew. It was this demotion, this enforced return to a past she had left behind. Her mind was sharp, honed by years of profiling some of the most dangerous minds, but now she would sift through the remnants of long-cold trails with little hope of solving them.

"Dammit," she whispered into the silence, her voice carrying a blend of defiance and resignation. A brilliant agent, benched. For Carly, the BAU wasn't just a job—it was where she excelled, where she belonged. And though she understood the necessity of consequences, it didn't ease the sting. Not one bit.

Her eyes narrowed as she stared out into the night. This city—with its clashing sirens of murmurs and whispers, its underbelly of secrets—was all too familiar. Carly wouldn't just fade into the background. No, she'd burn through every case they threw at her until the flames of her tenacity and skill lit the way back to where she deserved to be.

She leaned over from the chair and grabbed her bag, retrieving a few things from it. Her fingers hovered over the phone, the device cold and unyielding under her touch. The screen lit up with an intensity that seemed to mock her hesitation. She could almost hear Justin's voice, a familiar baritone tinged with the accent of their shared Chicago upbringing. It would be so easy to dial his number, to bridge the years of silence with a simple call. He was so mad at her the last time they had spoken.

But memories clawed at her resolve—a bitter cocktail of childhood rivalries and a family fractured beyond easy repair. Recklessness had cost Carly her place in the BAU; she wouldn't let it cost her what little peace she had scraped together since then. With a sharp exhale, she set the phone down.

No, not yet.

There were other ghosts she needed to confront first—those ensnared within the pages of cold case files, waiting for her keen eye to give them voice once more. And they would wait until morning. But Carly's mind would not.

The apartment was spartan, a temporary bastion against the chaos of the city. Carly found solace in its bareness, the lack of personal touches a reflection of her current state: transient, searching. Tonight, she filled the space with the rustle of old papers as she prepped for her first day on the Cold Case unit.

Her kitchen table became an altar to the forgotten, each case file a scripture of loss and yearning. The beam from her desk lamp cast long shadows across photographs that whispered of lives snatched away, leaving behind only questions. She traced the outline of one photo—a young woman, her smile forever frozen in time before fate had swept her off into obscurity.

"Emily Rosario," Carly murmured, committing the name to memory. She wasn't just chasing killers; she was chasing echoes, trying to piece together the fragments they left behind. Each file was a challenge, a dare to see if she could outwit the shroud of time that had cloaked these crimes in mystery, and to give families closure who had for too long waited in grief.

She flipped through pages lined with notes from detectives who had long since given up or moved on. The ink faded, but the desperation was still palpable. Carly's eyes were steel blue lighthouses cutting through the fog of forgotten details and dead ends.

"Tomorrow, we start again," Carly said out loud to the apartment, holding the files, wondering what the next day—her first day on the job—would bring.

CHAPTER THREE

Carly stepped into the Chicago field office with a tempered resolve, the polished floor reflecting the glare of office lights above. A demotion from the BAU to Cold Cases was not what she'd envisioned for her career, yet here she was, in the city where her past loomed as large as the steel and glass towers outside.

The air in the office was heavy with the musk of old paper and the faint buzz of fluorescent lights. Desks were islands in a sea of gray carpet, each with their own stacks of files, their own little histories of violence and loss. It was a far cry from the high-adrenaline chase that had landed her in this quiet purgatory. That recklessness, the rush of the hunt—it seemed a world away now.

She navigated the maze of cubicles, her keen eyes taking in everything: the agents hunched over their desks, the aloof nod of acknowledgment toward her presence, the subtle shift of papers as if to conceal ongoing work from the new arrival. Carly belonged there, she told herself that, even if it didn't feel quite true yet.

She walked over to the doorway of a small office and stood there for a moment.

"Agent Phoenix?" The voice cut through her inspection, causing Carly to pivot on her heel.

Michael Grayson stood before her, his expression an unreadable mask. An old colleague had told Carly about what to expect. "Gray" people called him, and Carly could see why; his demeanor was as neutral as his name, his eyes a flat, steely hue that felt like wells of repression. He was older, perhaps in his late forties, the lines on his face etched by years of service, and his posture spoke of a man who took pride in his work—a man who followed rules. Carly didn't like the rules, and she knew that could be a problem.

"Agent Grayson?" Carly greeted him, extending a hand that he took after a moment's hesitation. His grip was firm but perfunctory, a formality rather than a welcome.

"Welcome to Cold Cases," he said, his tone devoid of enthusiasm. "I heard about your last case. I hope you're ready to slow down. Cold cases are a little different from what you've been used to."

"Slowing down isn't really my style," Carly replied, a hint of defiance in her voice, despite knowing full well that she needed to make this work. The tension between them stretched taut, a silent acknowledgment of the chasm of their differing approaches to the job.

"Let's hope you can adapt then," Gray remarked, his gaze lingering on her for a moment before he turned back to his desk. Carly watched him go, his steps measured and precise, the antithesis of the chaos she'd left behind.

Carly leaned against the doorjamb of Gray's office, her arms folded, an attempt at casual ease betrayed by the rigidity of her posture. The room was a testament to Gray's methodical nature—everything in its place, the scent of aged paper and black coffee intermingling to create an almost sacred ambiance. She cleared her throat softly, trying to pierce the silence that had settled between them since their introduction.

"Look, Agent Gray," she began, her tone carefully modulated to convey sincerity, "Can I call you Gray? I know this isn't ideal for either of us, and you have your way of doing things, but I'm here to do *my* part. Maybe we can find some common ground."

Gray didn't look up from his paperwork. His pen continued to scratch out notes with a deliberateness that seemed designed to exclude her. "Common ground is built on mutual respect, Agent Phoenix," he said without warmth. "Respect is earned, not assumed."

She bit back a retort, the words 'mutual respect' echoing in her mind like a challenge. Her reputation had preceded her, and Gray's walls were already up. Carly wasn't used to being on the defensive, but if she was going to survive in this new role, she would have to navigate around Gray's skepticism.

"Fair enough," she conceded, pushing off from the doorway, and likewise pushing away her desire to fight fire with fire.

Carly stepped further into the room, her gaze drifting across the landscape of Gray's workspace. It was orderly, each file and artifact placed with intention. Her eyes landed on an old newspaper clipping pinned under a glass paperweight, the edges yellowed with age. The headline was partially obscured, but the date stood out, harking back to a time when she was just a kid in this very city.

A second desk sat with case files on it. Carly knew instinctively that it was her own.

Curiosity piqued, Carly approached the desk, though she felt like an interloper encroaching on sacred ground. She reached out tentatively, her fingertips brushing the cool surface of the paperweight. Beneath it, the grainy photograph of a young woman she recognized stared back at her, frozen in time. It was the same picture she had seen in the cold cases she had looked at the day before.

Carly could feel the hum of a story there, one that had been left dangling on the precipice of obscurity.

"Emily Rosario," she murmured, reading the name aloud without realizing it. The room seemed to grow colder with the utterance, as if the mention of the long-gone woman stirred something restless.

"An old case?" Carly asked, knowing the answer, glancing over her shoulder at Gray, who finally looked up, his expression an enigmatic mask that offered no clues to his thoughts. There was a flicker in his eyes, though, a brief spark that suggested this was more than just another file to him.

Carly pulled out an attached file and then slid out an article beside it. The print had faded to a soft gray, like whispers of smoke, and the paper crackled as if it might crumble to dust with just a bit more provocation. She unfolded the clipping with reverence, her movements deliberate, not wanting to further fray its fragile edges.

"Local Diner Waitress Murdered After Midnight Shift" was emblazoned across the top in a bold type that belied the cold case's dormancy. Carly's eyes flickered over the text, absorbing the story of a young Emily Rosario who'd clocked out from a late shift at a greasy spoon called The Silver Spoon Diner and stepped into the Chicago night, never to be seen alive again.

"Taken?" she whispered to herself, picturing the unguarded back exit of a diner that she knew all too well, the kind of place that clung to the shadows of the city.

The article recounted witness statements: fleeting images of a petite figure slipping into an old truck, exhaust fumes blending with the chill of early morning air, the driver nothing more than a silhouette against the dim glow of streetlights. The article noted, with detached precision, how Emily's body was later discovered in a bloody grave at a small stretch of woodland beside Lake Michigan outside of city bounds, frozen solid.

The lack of leads was almost as disturbing as the crime itself. No suspect had ever been identified, no motive unearthed. Just a void where Emily's future should have been. Carly felt the stirrings of the familiar fire within her—the drive to unravel the tangled threads that others had abandoned, or worse, failed to see.

"Forty years," Carly mused, her mind racing through the

advancements in forensics since Emily's death. "Someone got away with murder."

Picking up the rest of the file, Carly's fingers brushed against the grain of the paper, its edges softened by time. She could almost feel the years that had passed since Emily Rosario's name first landed on a missing person's report, her life distilled into ink and pulp. She thought about her mom and dad, how they would have been around at that time, doing their best but failing badly, only to have kids and then fail even worse.

In her gut, she knew that stepping into Chicago's pat would bring her closer to her own demons. But it was her job, and she felt a great sense of duty to do what was needed.

Straightening up in the chair that wasn't yet hers, she cast a glance around Gray's workspace. It was meticulous, sterile, a stark contrast to the chaos that so often accompanied cases like Emily's.

Gray was continuing his work without paying Carly much attention.

Carly decided with a precision that felt surgical, staring at the open file. "I'm taking this one," Carly announced. There was no grandeur in her voice, no promise of easy victories. Only the certainty of someone who knew that her path and Emily's had intersected for a reason.

Gray looked up. "The Rosario case? Be my guest."

"Emily Rosario," she whispered, her gaze fixed on the faded photograph clipped among the files. The girl's smile was hauntingly vibrant, a moment captured before darkness swallowed her whole. Carly felt the weight of responsibility settle upon her shoulders, an oath taken without witnesses. She looked around the room at the filing cabinets and wondered how many people had been left forgotten within them. A great sadness fell across her like an icy wind.

She would not let Emily's story be reduced to a forgotten file; she would chase the truth until it bled daylight.

As if acknowledging her resolve, the air conditioning kicked in with a suddenness that sent an icy embrace down her spine. Carly wrapped her arms around herself, the chill not entirely born from the blast of cold air.

Gray stared at her. He nodded. "If you need some help with that one…"

"Thank you," she said politely, though uncertain Agent Gray really meant it.

She stared down at the file.

It was a lonesome road, a cold case—a place where time stood sentinel over secrets and regrets. But Carly had seen enough tragedy in her life. She was no stranger to the desolation of such paths. She'd walk it, as many times as it took, to bring Emily's murderer to justice.

"You have my number, if you need me," Carly said, taking her coat.

"Where are you heading first?" Gray asked, an eyebrow raised.

"To where it all began," she answered gravely.

CHAPTER FOUR

Carly's breath formed a white mist before her as she stepped cautiously onto the icy shore of Lake Michigan, where years ago, the frozen body of Emily Rosario had been discovered. The wind sliced through her jacket, biting at her skin with relentless ferocity. Her boots crunched over the frosty gravel and patches of snow; each step seemed to be lost against the silence of the vast, desolate waterfront. Under her arm was a paper envelope containing photographs.

Tucking a stray strand of blonde hair behind her ear, Carly's gaze swept over the horizon where steely waters met the gray winter sky. Somewhere nearby, Emily Rosario had been left a bludgeoned corpse. Here, amid the stillness, there was no escaping the oppressive presence of death that hung in the air. She imagined the scene as it was in the past: an unsuspecting sheet of snow disrupted violently by the outline of a fallen figure, the palette of a life once vibrant now subdued into the pallor of the void.

Her eyes narrowed, focusing on the precise location detailed in the reports, where the ice had been disturbed next to a tree line, where the land had reluctantly given up its grim secret. A shiver ran through her that wasn't from the cold alone. It was as if the memory of Emily whispered across the expanse, settling on Carly's conscience with a weightless yet undeniable touch.

The connection surged through her veins. Emily, an aspiring artist, petite and full of life, had vanished into the night only to reemerge in this grim setting, her potential forever silenced. Carly felt that loss acutely, as though the echoes of Emily's dreams were mingling with her own suppressed aspirations. She knew the sting of having one's path abruptly altered, her recent demotion a dim parallel. But here, Carly stood on the precipice of something important, something that could not only redefine her career but also give Emily the acknowledgment she deserved.

"Stabbed 13 times," she murmured into the chill, looking at the ground, imagining the virgin snow tinged with red.

Looking at the photographs, Carly noticed a large boulder that was present near the crime scene and could infer the exact spot where Emily had been found.

Carly kneeled beside the spot, an invisible imprint left by a body long since removed, her breath forming brief clouds of frozen air against the steely backdrop of Lake Michigan. The crime scene photos fanned out before her were an unsettling mosaic of blue and white—the color of death's cruel artistry. With gloved fingers, she traced the edges of each image, her eyes darting from glossy paper to the barren shore, as if the answers might be etched somewhere between.

"Was it someone you knew?" Carly whispered, the name tasting of resolve on her lips. "Why did you get into that truck?"

Carly knew the driver had never been identified. That didn't mean he was the killer, but it was a safe bet he knew more than anyone else. After all, killer or not, he may have been the last person to see her alive.

She shuffled through the pictures methodically in the cold, noting how the shadows fell across the snow in each, how the ice seemed to cradle Emily's form with deceptive tenderness. The photos were silent sentinels to the violence that had occurred, but Carly was listening for the discordant note, the detail that sang out of tune with the rest.

It was then that something caught her eye in the photos—a dusting of snow on some nearby branches. She wondered if the killer's footsteps were hidden by it all those years ago, and any possible blood trail. Forensics had moved on markedly in forty years, and Carly knew she couldn't rely on everything in the files. All information had to be examined with care in case something had been missed.

"Were you killed here, Emily? Or did the killer dump you here on the ice?" Carly asked the still lake. But only the wind returned an answer.

The realization unfurled like a flag in her mind: the case wasn't cold, it was waiting—waiting for someone to peer beneath the surface. Carly stood up, her stature unyielding against the biting wind. Her mind swirled with thoughts as she stood on the desolate shore, the memory of Emily Rosario lingering like a phantasm. She envisioned Emily's vibrant spirit, her artistic dreams abruptly cut short by a brutal end. The contrast of red blood against pristine snow painted a stark picture in Carly's imagination, a chilling reminder of the violence that had stained this serene landscape.

Could Emily's killer have been an artist too? Carly pondered the possibility, considering the eerie choice of location where the body was left as a macabre form of artistic expression. The idea sent shivers through her, the notion of a murderer using death as their canvas both disturbing and intriguing.

A burning desire ignited within Carly, fueling her need to return to the office and delve deeper into the case files. She yearned to uncover any overlooked clues or connections that could shed light on Emily's tragic fate. With each step back towards her car, determination etched into her features, Carly knew that she was inching closer to unraveling the mysteries surrounding Emily's murder.

As Carly turned away from the desolate shore, a gust of wind whipped through her, carrying with it a sense of the past. She paused, her breath hanging in the frigid air like a visible whisper. The barren landscape stretched out before her, a silent witness to the tragedy that had unfolded there decades ago.

In that moment, Carly felt a profound sadness wash over her—a weighty ache that settled deep within her chest. She couldn't shake the image of Emily's lifeless form sprawled on the icy ground, a stark contrast against the pristine snow. The realization of all that Emily had lost, all the dreams left unfulfilled, pierced Carly's heart with a sharp pang. Carly, in her own way, knew the feeling of being forgotten.

The windswept expanse seemed to hold its breath, as if waiting for closure that had eluded it for so long. Carly's gaze lingered on the spot where tragedy had struck, an invisible marker of loss etched into the very fabric of the land.

Turning away reluctantly, Carly pulled up her collar against the wind and headed back to her car.

*

Carly's fingers tightened around the steering wheel, the leather groaning softly under her grip. The city blurred past her window, a mosaic of shadows and light that flickered like an old film reel. She drove with purpose, the engine's steady thrum a bass line to the cacophony of Chicago's heartbeat.

Buildings rose and fell in her peripheral vision, but Carly's focus remained tunnel-vision sharp on the image seared into her mind: Emily Rosario's face, now an avatar of unanswered questions. Each red light was a brief pause in her mental replay of the crime scene, each green a signal to race towards the truth.

The FBI field office loomed ahead, its facade an unyielding curtain against the dusky sky. Carly parked with precision, her movements mechanical yet charged with energy. She locked her car and walked briskly on the concrete—a metronome ticking down the time they had lost and the time she had to reclaim.

Inside, the office hummed with subdued intensity. Agents moved through the fluorescent-lit space, their conversations hushed but fervent. Carly bypassed them all, her eyes fixed on the door to Gray's, and her, office.

She entered the room, Agent Gray nowhere to be seen, the scent of old paper and polish greeting her. The case files were neatly stacked, relics of bygone battles against crime. Carly's hand moved over them before halting at one labeled 'Rosario, Emily.'

With a slow inhale, Carly opened the file. Photographs spilled out, glossy reminders of a life extinguished too soon. Every image was a piece of the puzzle—frozen expressions, landscapes caught in time, the subtle play of shadow and light on snow.

As she sifted through the documents, Carly's mind worked in overdrive, drawing connections, mapping possibilities. Notes were scrawled in margins, overlooked details begging for attention. Her fingers traced the edges of the photographs, as if contact could bridge the gap between now and then, agent and victim.

Carly's eyes narrowed as she leafed through the dusty case file, her gaze snagging on a detail previously dismissed as inconsequential. An offhand mention of a key card found at the scene, thought to be irrelevant, now burned with potential. It was from a nearby hotel—a place Emily Rosario had no reason to visit. The original detectives had checked for connections, but their inquiry was superficial at best.

"Maybe you weren't just a lost girl in the wrong place," Carly whispered to the photos. She scribbled a note to check the hotel's records again—this time for any employees or guests who might have slipped through the cracks of the initial investigation. "Maybe you planned to meet the driver…"

She turned the page, and another piece of information caught her eye. A small, almost invisible bruise on the inside of Emily's forearm, documented but never explored—marked as an incidental finding. Yet Carly saw a pattern there, one that spoke not of random happenstance, but of practiced control. A grip too firm to be friendly, too precise to be accidental.

Was this from him leading you to your death? Carly thought. If that were the case, then she was either at gunpoint or unaware she was about to die. There would have been a bigger struggle had Emily thought she would be killed.

Carly started to think that Emily trusted the killer, at least enough to think he wouldn't truly harm her.

"Who wanted to keep you close?" she pondered, the question hanging in the air. Determination settled in her jaw as she made another note, this time to cross-reference this overlooked clue with known methods of assailants who exerted subtle force. The gloom of the room seemed to deepen, wrapping around her, urging her closer to the precipice of the unknown.

The silence of the office was pierced by the sound of Carly's steady breaths as she delved deeper into the archives. She logged into her computer and searched the database. A thought had occurred to her, another thread to pull. She shuffled through reports, witness statements, and blurry photocopies until a particular case file commanded her attention.

The name of the victim was emblazoned upon it—Jennings, Sarah.

In Carly's work with serial killers, she had found several who had been nomadic, moving from town to town. This made them difficult to track down. She wondered if the truck driver was just such a man. If so, then could another murder be attributed to him? One that would reveal new leads.

Sarah Jennings had a similar bruise on her arm and had been stabbed 13 times, just like Emily. And her body had been frozen solid from the cold weather.

As Carly pored over the details, an icy thread of recognition entered her mind. Sarah Jennings was last seen leaving an office party, her vibrant red hair a beacon that vanished into the winter night. Her body was later discovered, posed like a macabre sculpture on the frozen ground.

There had been a preliminary investigation into whether Sarah and Emily's deaths had been connected, but it seemed that hadn't bore fruit. Carly understood that. Detective work was hard, and not everything turned out the way you wanted it to.

"Too similar," Carly murmured, as the parallels with Emily Rosario's case materialized before her. Both victims were young, full of promise, their lives snuffed out during the cruelest of winters. The same deliberate positioning of the bodies, the same absence of struggle. It was as if the killer sought to preserve their final moments in ice.

"Are you his art?" Carly questioned the still faces in the crime scene photos. The uncanny resemblance of the poses created an icy atmosphere that wasn't entirely due to the chill of the room.

She reached for the phone to contact archives, her fingers poised above the keypad. It was time to bring these women out of the cold shadows of forgotten files.

CHAPTER FIVE

Carly's eyes narrowed as she scrutinized the frayed edges of the case file in front of her. She had been down in the archives all day, looking for files that weren't scanned into the database. Her fingers, dusted with the residue of time and neglect, flipped through the pages detailing Sarah Jennings' life and untimely death. The sterile glow of the office did little to warm the chill that settled over Carly as she delved deeper into the forgotten notes and files of the cold case.

"Sarah Jennings," she murmured under her breath, absorbing every word as if it were a lifeline cast across the years. The 28-year-old's ambitions had been snuffed out like a flame in the dead of night, her vibrant red hair and striking features now just faded memories captured in grainy photographs and police sketches.

It had happened just 6 months after the death of Emily.

The similarities between Sarah's demise and the Rosario case nipped at the back of Carly's mind, persistent and gnawing. Both women had been plucked from the safety of their lives, leaving behind nothing but questions swirling in the void they left. Both women had been stabbed 13 times, and both had similar small bruises on their arms.

As Carly aligned the timelines, the coincidences began to stack up, forming a pattern that couldn't be ignored.

"Left alone, no immediate suspects," Carly said to the empty room, listing the details aloud as if to cement them in reality.

Her gaze darted across autopsy reports, crime scene photos, and witness statements, piecing together a puzzle that had long been abandoned. The killer had been meticulous, leaving behind a vacuum where evidence should have been, but Carly could read between the lines—the void itself was a clue.

"Same MO..." she trailed off, her mind racing ahead of her words.

Photos of the victims laid side by side seemed to whisper secrets only Carly could hear, their silent pleas for justice fueling her resolve. The scent of old paper filled her lungs as she leaned closer, her light hair falling like a curtain around her focused gaze.

Carly knew she'd need to investigate the scene where Sarah had been killed.

But she also knew chasing down two murder cases on her first day was stretching things. She'd need help. Someone who could help her chase down multiple leads. She headed up from the basement where the archives were held and headed back to her new office.

Grayson sat at his desk, a mountain of case files surrounding him like a fortress of the past. His brow furrowed in concentration as he meticulously reviewed witness statements from a decades-old robbery. The soft glow of the desk lamp cast long shadows across his weathered face, emphasizing the lines etched by years spent chasing dead ends and cold cases.

Carly's entrance disrupted the quiet hum of the office, her presence a whirlwind of determination and purpose. She stood tall before Grayson, her eyes ablaze with an unspoken urgency that tugged at something buried deep within him.

"Gray," Carly's voice cut through the silence, carrying with it a hint of desperation wrapped in steel. "I need your expertise on another case. It might be connected to Emily Rosario's."

Grayson raised an eyebrow, his expression guarded as he glanced up from the file spread out before him. His initial reluctance was evident, rooted in his dedication to methodical work and reluctance to deviate from his established routine.

"I have my own workload," Grayson replied evenly, his tone betraying none of the curiosity that flickered behind his steady gaze.

Carly leaned closer, her voice lowering to a persuasive whisper that echoed with sincerity. "This is my first case here, Gray. I need someone who knows their way around these old files and can see what I might miss."

A flicker of uncertainty danced across Grayson's features before being swiftly replaced by a mask of professional detachment.

With a resigned sigh, Grayson closed the file before him and rose from his chair with deliberate grace. The weight of experience settled upon his shoulders like an old cloak as he met Carly's unwavering gaze.

"Lead the way," he said simply.

*

Carly stepped out of the unmarked sedan, the crunch of snow beneath her breaking the silence that hung over the desolate field. The winter sun was a weak bystander, offering little warmth or clarity to the scene before her. Gray followed, his breath materializing in puffs of white as he closed the car door with a soft thud.

“Here?” Gray asked, skepticism threading his voice like an unwelcome undercurrent.

“Exactly here,” Carly confirmed, scanning the empty stretch of land where Sarah Jennings’ life had been stolen from her years ago. There was nothing to see now but the skeletal remains of trees bordering the area and the endless gray sky above them. Carly was struck by the similarity to where Emily had been left. The treeline and a flat valley stretching out, was eerily similar to the treeline by Lake Michigan.

“Hard to imagine sometimes,” Gray said, his words laced with an unintentional coldness that matched the surrounding air. “So much time has passed, you can never be certain of anything on these cases.”

Carly walked with purpose, her mind reconstructing the crime scene from the faded photographs she had studied meticulously back at the office. Each step felt heavy with the gravity of what had occurred on this forgotten patch of earth. She envisioned where Sarah’s body must have lain, the crimson stain of blood on snow now long absorbed by time and elements.

“Both victims were found in open spaces by a line of trees, left exposed to the elements. It’s theatrical, in a morbid sense,” Carly mused aloud, her thoughts crystalline despite the biting chill.

“Could be coincidence,” Gray countered, ever the voice of reason. “It doesn’t take a genius killer to pick two isolated spots near trees.”

“Or it could be a signature,” Carly shot back, her gaze still locked on the invisible outline of the past. “And their looks—striking and vibrant. They stood out, they were seen.”

“You’d need more than that,” Gray said, quietly.

"How about both being stabbed 13 times," Carly said. She then fished out two printouts of the bodies. "And look here, they both had similar bruises on their arms."

“How did that get missed?” Gray asked, sounding annoyed.

“How many murders have there been out here?” Carly said, remembering the trickle of deaths reported in the area from when she was a kid. “It’s easy to case both away as unrelated. Whatever the case is, both girls were seen by someone. I don’t think they were targeted by accident.”

“Seen by the wrong person,” Gray added quietly, his eyes reflecting a depth of understanding that suggested his skepticism was starting to wane.

"Exactly," Carly said, feeling the pieces click into place within her. She turned to face Gray, her expression etched with certainty. "We're looking for someone who preys on visibility, on life being lived loudly. Someone who wants to snuff out that brightness."

Gray's voice carried a weight of reminiscence as he recounted the past, his eyes distant as if peering into a time long gone. "Back when I was just starting out, we were after this guy, Dean Williams. He had a taste for taking young women's lives. Three of them before we even caught a whiff of him." His words hung in the air like a frozen painting.

Carly's curiosity sparked, and she turned to Gray, her gaze wide with intrigue. "Who managed to piece it together?" she inquired, eager to unravel the mystery behind Gray's early triumph.

A flicker of pride gleamed in Gray's gaze as he met Carly's inquisitive stare. "It was me," he confessed with quiet confidence, his tone tinged with modesty. "My superiors didn't believe me at first. So… Perhaps we shouldn't so readily disregard your theory that it's the same killer."

The sun dipped lower on the horizon, casting long shadows across the snow-covered landscape as Carly and Gray continued their investigation.

"Let's walk the perimeter," she suggested, already stepping forward, her mind a whirlwind of theories and patterns. Gray followed, his own mental gears shifting, beginning to align with Carly's unorthodox yet undeniably sharp detective skills.

Carly crouched low, her gaze sweeping the now barren field where, years ago, Sarah Jennings' life had been cruelly discarded. A chill wind skittered across the landscape, brushing against Carly's face as if mocking her efforts to resurrect secrets from this frozen graveyard. The sun dipped lower, surrendering its throne to the encroaching blanket of twilight that threatened to obscure her search.

Carly's fingers traced the edges of the printouts in her hand, the images of Sarah and Emily's lifeless bodies stark against the white backdrop. She held them up side by side, aligning the angles of the crime scenes with precision.

"Look at this, Gray," she urged, her voice steady with conviction. "The way Sarah's body was positioned in relation to these trees—it mirrors how Emily was placed near the lake. It's like he's composing his own twisted art piece. But it's the same perspective."

Gray studied the photographs intently, his brow furrowed in thought. "You think he's creating some kind of painting with each victim?" he mused aloud, catching onto Carly's train of deduction.

“More than that,” Carly affirmed, her gaze flickering between the pictures as if seeking obscured clues within their frozen frames. “There’s a meticulousness to it—a deliberate placement that goes beyond mere disposal. That tells me the killer had something specific in his mind. An image he was trying to reproduce. The killer could be re-enacting his first kill, or he could be disposing of the bodies in this way, trying to recreate a memory that’s important to him. Even a famous painting or scene from a film.”

“It’s an interesting idea. But we should try to figure out any other connections between the victims. We need to dig deeper into their lives before they were taken,” Gray suggested, his tone shifting from skepticism to collaboration. “See if there are any threads connecting them beyond this grim symmetry. Did they know each other, move in the same circles, etc?”

“Yeah, it’s a good place to start,” Carly said, still unable to remove the image of the two bodies from her mind. It had to be more than a coincidence. It *had* to be. But she suspected Gray was a by-the-numbers, procedural agent. And there was merit in that, too, beyond Carly's intuitive techniques.

“Let’s get going,” Carly said.

The sun dipped lower on the horizon, casting a crimson glow over the wintry landscape as Carly and Gray walked back to their car.

“You never know,” Cary said. “We might get lucky. The connection could be the killer himself. And his identity could be sitting in those dusty archives.”

They moved off, not saying much on the drive home, both strangers to each other—but strangers with a singular purpose: To catch a killer who had evaded capture for decades.

CHAPTER SIX

Carly leaned over the sprawl of cold case files, her hair cascading like a pale waterfall onto the dimly lit desk. The Chicago Field Office had an air of faded diligence, its walls lined with shelving that bore the weight of unsolved mysteries, each binder on them a silent scream for closure. She felt the spectral presence of Sarah Jennings and Emily Rosario in the room, their young lives snuffed out and frozen in time within the case files.

Already, Carly could feel how easy it would be to be taken over by cold cases.

"Gray," Carly's voice broke the silence, "how often do these old cases actually get solved?"

Gray looked up from his own stack of papers. His eyes were windows to a mind that had seen too many dead ends, yet they held a spark that refused to be extinguished by the bleak reality of unsolved crimes. He was a traditionalist, rooted in procedure, his answers always measured and cautious. Carly could sense this about him, but underneath, she felt something else simmering. What that was, she was yet to discover.

"Truth? More often than not, they stay cold," Gray responded, his voice steady but tinged with something Carly recognized as regret.

A momentary shadow crossed Carly's face, eyes reflecting a flicker of doubt that she quickly quashed. Gray seemed to notice; he seemed good at noticing things—a skill no doubt honed by years of navigating the obscure trenches of forgotten cases. He straightened slightly, offering a small nod of encouragement.

"Doesn't mean we don't try, Phoenix. Every case cracked started out just like this."

"Right," Carly said quietly, buoyed somewhat by his words. She turned her attention back to the files, her analytical mind dissecting every detail, searching for the thread that would unravel the knot of mystery. "How long have you been at this?"

"Two decades with the Bureau," Gray replied. "About twelve on cold cases."

Carly sensed Gray getting a little uncomfortable with the congenial chat, and so she turned her attentions elsewhere.

"Anything yet?" Gray asked.

"I'm just looking over the timelines before both murders," Carly explained. "If there was a connection, we might find it in their... Bingo!"

Gray looked up, not even breaking a smile. "What is it?"

As she sifted through the timelines of the victims' last known activities, a pattern began to surface, a coincidence too stark to ignore.

"Both Sarah and Emily, in the days leading up to their respective murders, had been patrons at a place called 'Art déco'." Carly frowned, the name unfamiliar. "That's got to mean something. It can't surely be a coincidence?"

"You'd be surprised," Gray said. "I had a case once where two men, Bill Carney and Robert Howard, they met up at a bar one night in a small town in the South. They have a few drinks, leave separately, and each went home and killed their wives."

"Some sort of pact?" Carly asked.

"You'd have thought that," Gray answered. "It turned out the two men had never met before. They were just crossing paths. According to a third bar fly who had been part of their night, Bill and Robert had spoken about baseball all night. Not one mention of their wives or even being violent. Just a pure coincidence. Nothing more."

Carly knew that Gray was right. Coincidences weren't enough to prove a connection between the victims. But she felt in her gut that there was more to this new lead than a random similarity.

"Art Deco?" she pondered aloud, more to herself than to Gray.

Gray glanced over, his expression unreadable as ever. "I know it. It's a cafe-bar hybrid, got a little exhibition space upstairs. Been around for over half a century. Quite the place for budding artists in the community."

"Still running?" Carly asked, interest piqued. Her mind already raced ahead, conjuring images of a time-worn establishment, the sort of place that held secrets in its very walls.

"Yes, I believe so," Gray confirmed. "Could be nothing, but it's a lead. And leads on a cold case are like gold dust."

"Then that's our next stop," Carly decided with renewed determination, feeling the tendrils of the case pulling her in deeper. She closed the file in front of her with a sense of purpose, ready to confront the past head-on at Art déco.

Gray stood up.

"I thought you had too much work to help me with this case?" Carly asked.

"I do," Gray answered. "But…"

"I don't need anyone to hold my hand."

"I didn't mean that," Gray said. "But if we can solve two murders in our stack of cold cases at once, that will help ease both of our burdens."

Carly and Gray gathered their coats, the weight of the unsolved cases lingering in the air around them like an unseen presence. As they exited the dimly lit office, the hallway lights flickered overhead, casting eerie shadows on the worn linoleum floor. They walked in silence towards the elevator, their footsteps echoing faintly in the empty corridor. The doors slid open with a soft hiss, revealing a small, cramped space that seemed to swallow them whole as they stepped inside.

The elevator descended with the sluggishness of machinery that had seen better decades, its groan a soundtrack to their silent anticipation. Carly's mind churned with theories and questions as the numbers on the panel flickered downward. Beside her, Gray shifted his weight subtly, the fabric of his coat whispering against itself.

"Your hunch... about these women," Gray broke the silence, his voice low but certain, "Well spotted."

Carly nodded, taking the short compliment from Gray as a rare treasure. She felt the corners of her lips tilt in a small, satisfied smile. The praise was unexpected, yet it stoked the fire within her, the relentless drive to prove herself not just to him, but to the haunted wraiths of her past mistakes.

The elevator dinged its arrival to the ground floor, its doors creaking open to release them into the dimming light of the Chicago afternoon. They stepped out, their footsteps syncing as they made their way to the car.

*

Art déco revealed itself as an anachronism amidst the modern storefronts lining the street, its façade a faded mural of times long gone. The sign above the door swayed gently in a cold Chicago breeze, the letters curling with the flair of a bygone era. Carly's gaze swept over it, absorbing the details—the peeling paint, the art nouveau lamps flanking the entrance, the window display crowded with eclectic artifacts and paintings reaching for relevance.

“Have you been here before?” Carly asked.

“A couple of times,” Gray answered.

"Really?" Carly smiled. "And I thought you were straight-laced."

“I am,” Gray said. “I was working.”

Gray opened the door, and Carly followed.

Inside, the scent of aged wood and oil paint hung heavily, a tangible presence that whispered stories of artists who once considered this their sanctuary. Carly’s eyes adjusted to the subdued lighting, taking in the walls crowded with framed pieces, the mismatched furniture that filled the space with a bohemian charm. A jazz record played softly, its melancholic notes floating through the air like wistful memories.

At the counter, an elderly man surveyed them with cautious curiosity from behind thick-rimmed glasses that magnified his keen eyes. His attire was as eccentric as his surroundings—velvet waistcoat over a paisley shirt, a scarf draped around his neck despite the indoor warmth.

“Mr. Fleming?” Carly ventured, her voice steady despite the flutter of her pulse. This place, this man—they were keys to unlocking the truth she sought.

“Indeed,” Fleming replied, his tone guarded. “Can I help you?”

“I’m Agent Grayson, this is Agent Phoenix,” Gray said, brandishing his badge like a robot who had done so a thousand times over.

Mr. Fleming looked a little startled.

“You’re the owner of Art déco, aren’t you?” Carly asked.

“Yes,” came the curt answer. “And we are preparing for an exhibition this evening, so please, can you tell me what this is all about?”

“We’re investigating a double homicide from forty years ago,” Gray offered.

Fleming nodded. “Well, I don’t know what I can do to help with that sort of thing. My memory isn’t the best, that’s why I write everything down.”

“Mr. Fleming!” a voice shouted from the back. “Should the Marcus watercolor go on the back wall?”

Mr. Fleming put his head in his hands for a second. “If I’ve told that boy a thousand times…” he murmured before shouting. “The East wall! Next to the D’leure!”

“I’m sorry, who was murdered?” Mr. Fleming asked, his attention clearly divided.

“Two people who frequented your bar,” Gray said, sternly. “Emily Rosario and Sarah Jennings. 1985 and 86, respectively.”

"Ah… I vaguely remember that," he said. "But it was a long time ago, and I don't think I have much to add. I really am quite busy today."

"We're looking into..." Carly began, but then she saw it—the flicker of disinterest in Fleming's eyes, the subtle retreat behind a wall of polite detachment. She needed a way in, a crack in his armor.

"Actually," she interjected smoothly, thinking fast. "I've always admired this place. My great uncle used to talk about it all the time—Danton Mulaney? He was an artist around here."

Fleming's demeanor transformed as if Carly had spoken a magic word. "Danton Mulaney?" he repeated, animated. "Oh my, a wonderful artist! He was quite the character. Had a few of his pieces upstairs once, wish I had held onto them as they are now worth a fortune." He gestured vaguely toward the ceiling, where the exhibition space lurked unseen.

"Did you know him well?" Carly pressed, sensing the opening she'd created.

"I brushed shoulders with him, but he was a truly international artist," Fleming said, but now he leaned forward, a spark of life igniting behind those old-world lenses. "Wouldn't it be wonderful if he were still around and here at Art déco today?" He sighed, seemingly slipping into a nostalgic mood.

Carly exchanged a glance with Gray, whose eyes told her she'd done well.

"Things really were better in the past, weren't they?" Carly continued. "I remember spending a lot of time with great uncle Danton, running around his feet as he painted. Long before cellphones and other intrusions."

"Oh my dear, you are correct," Fleming said. "We certainly have lost something with all of this 'progress'."

"Yes," Carly said. "Sometimes though, threads are left from the past, things unresolved. That's why we're here, to go back to the 80s and figure out what happened to Emily Rosario and Sarah Jennings."

Fleming's eyes lit up as if recognition had finally floated to the surface of his mind.

"Oh, yes," he said mournfully. "Now I do remember those names."

The dust motes danced in the slanted sunlight that filtered through Art déco's stained glass windows, like particles of time disturbed by the opening of long-sealed vaults. Carly felt it - this place was a mausoleum of memories, where echoes of the past whispered secrets if one listened closely enough.

"Emily Rosario," Fleming said, the name rolling off his tongue with a tinge of reverence and loss. "She was an artist and an excellent one. She had an eye for color and form that could've taken her far. But her training wasn't complete before she was sadly taken from us." He clasped his hands behind his back, eyes unfocused as if viewing paintings only he could see.

"And Sarah Jennings?" Carly prompted, her voice slicing through the stillness of retrospection.

Fleming's gaze snapped back to the present. "Ah, Sarah. She wasn't one of us, not an artist. But she came here, bought pieces now and then. She liked to surround herself with beauty, I suppose. Business people often like to appear multi-dimensional, and so they either hang expensive artworks in their offices to project power and depth, or they want to have their pictures taken for the press, showing their donations to the artistic world, for all to see. Sarah was most definitely in the latter category.

"The reason I do remember her to a degree is that Art déco had a bit of financial problems and she and her colleagues had some fundraisers for us from time to time. It did indeed help… Where would art be without its patrons?"

Gray leaned in, his voice carrying the weight of authority softened by genuine curiosity. "Do you think there's any connection between their murders?"

"Connection?" Fleming scoffed lightly, shaking his head. "No, I never saw them together, at least. This place draws all sorts - paths cross without ever really intertwining."

"Yet both found themselves at the end of the same dark road," Gray said, his words hanging in the air, heavy with implication. "If they were both here around that time, doesn't that make you think there could be a connection?

"Pure coincidence, detective. That's my belief," Fleming replied, though Carly noticed the slight falter in his conviction. "This is a place that breeds life and the exploration of life through art. Murder is the antithesis of that."

"Perhaps," Gray conceded but persisted, "could there have been an event? Something special that might have brought them both here at the same time where they could have encountered the same people?"

"You said you have to write everything down," Carly said. "You wouldn't happen to keep diaries or journals from that time?"

Fleming paused, considering. His eyes darted toward the staircase leading upstairs, and his mind seemed to travel with his gaze. "Wait here," he said abruptly and turned, his steps carrying a sense of purpose as he ascended the creaking stairs.

Carly watched him vanish into the shadows above, her adrenaline increasing. There was more to this than Fleming was letting on, and the key to unlocking it lay hidden amidst the relics of this venerable establishment. Every artist, every patron who passed through these doors left an imprint, however faint.

"Quite a thing, to be related to Danton Mulaney," Gray said in a low voice, the words infused with a hint of sarcasm. "His work was before my time, but I know he made quite the splash in the Chicago art scene."

Carly's lips twitched into a smile. She turned to Gray, catching the pale light of the overhead panels. "It was a lie," she confessed. "Never had an uncle named Danton or any other kind of Mulaney."

Gray's brows arched, a mild surprise etching into his otherwise unreadable expression. "That's not exactly by the book, Phoenix," he chided, though the corners of his mouth betrayed him with an almost imperceptible lift.

"Sometimes you've got to bend the rules to catch a break," Carly retorted, her gaze unapologetic. "And it got Fleming to open up, didn't it?"

"True enough," Gray conceded, his tone suggesting he might just be warming up to her unconventional tactics.

Quickly, the sound of footsteps descending a staircase caught their attention. Fleming appeared, clutching an aged diary, its leather cover worn by the years. Carly's heart gave a lurch of anticipation. That diary held secrets; she could feel it.

"Kept one every year," Fleming announced, holding the book like a sacred text. "Figured someone might find my life interesting after I'm gone, especially all my stories of artistic encounters."

"May we?" Gray asked, gesturing toward the diary.

"Of course, detective." Fleming handed it over, dusting off the cover.

"1985," Carly murmured, thumbing through the pages. Her mind raced—this was the year Emily Rosario had been killed, just before Sarah Jennings a few months later.

"Here," Fleming pointed, "a corporate meeting. Fleetover Ltd. Something about a fundraiser. Again, the only reason I remember it is that one of my partners got into bother financially and it was possible Art déco would go under. It was a very difficult time. Thank the gods, we got through it. Sarah Jennings and a few others helped raise donations, but the uncertainty of that time always gives me a horrible feeling of dread. I could have ended up in the gutter."

"And you think Emily Rosario might have been there as well?" Carly probed.

"It's very possible," Fleming said. "You see, we lent some pieces from upcoming local artists for the fundraiser to show how important our work was at fostering the next big thing. I believe Emily may have had a painting there, though I haven't noted that down. If she did, there's a good chance she was there. Artists crave the reaction of their audience, it's rare for them to turn down that opportunity."

"Did you attend this fundraiser?" Gray asked.

"Actually, according to the diary, I did not," Fleming answered. "We had an exhibition on and I had to keep appearances up that all was fine. My diary entry here says that my assistant at that time, Paul Ulsen attended."

"Can we speak with Paul Ulsen?" Carly asked.

"Dead for years now," Fleming replied, his voice carrying a note of finality. "A boating accident. A real shame as he was certainly better than some of the staff I have now." Fleming pointed upstairs.

"Does the company who held the fundraiser, Fleetover Ltd, still exist?" Gray inquired, his inquisitive nature kicking in.

"Way ahead of you," Carly said, showing the screen of her phone to reveal the address of a company that refused to die with the past. "Still active."

A spark ignited in Gray's eyes—recognition, perhaps, of Carly's razor-sharp acuity. They had a lead, a tangible thread in a case as old as the dust clinging to Fleming's diary.

Carly extended a hand to Fleming, the gesture an anchor in the reality of their mission. "Thank you for your help," she said, her voice steady despite the undercurrent of urgency that pulsed through her.

"Anytime," Fleming replied, his gaze lingered on Carly with a discernible flicker of old-world charm. "And Miss Phoenix, do come back and tell me all about Danton Mulaney. I would love to hear about what it was like to grow up around that kind of creativity!"

"Sure," Carly said, a half-truth slipping out as smoothly as the fabricated connection had earlier. She turned to leave, Gray's presence a silent force at her back.

They navigated through the maze of eclectic decor that was Art déco, stepping out into the crisp Chicago air which seemed to slice through the day's tension. The city hummed around them—a vast organism alive with secrets and stories.

"Are you planning on inventing more colorful ancestors?" Gray asked, the hint of a smile playing at the edge of his words. His traditionalist demeanor had softened, if only just.

"Only if it gets us leads," Carly quipped, matching his tone. "Besides, if Fleming calls my bluff, we'll just have to dress you up and pass you off as an enigmatic artist from a far-off land. That should keep him happy. You'll need a fake beard and mustache and an outrageous accent, though." Her eyes sparkled with mischief, a fleeting reprieve from the gravity of their task.

Gray shook his head, a quiet laugh escaping him. They reached the car, the unassuming government-issue sedan quite sterile compared to the vibrant life they'd just left inside Art déco.

As Carly slid behind the wheel, her mind shifted gears, already plotting their next move. She looked at the darkening sky above. The day would soon be coming to a close, and she already felt that they had covered a lot of ground like a yo-yo, but there was still time to squeeze more out of it.

"Let's see if Fleetover Ltd. has any record of that fundraiser," she said, firing up the engine. The dashboard lit up, casting a soft glow against the darkening sky outside, dimly lighting up the stoic figure of agent Grayson beside her.

CHAPTER SEVEN

The towering silhouette of Fleetwood LTD loomed over Carly as she and Gray approached the revolving doors. In its reflection, Chicago's steel-and-glass giants stood sentinel to the relentless pursuit within. The building was a monolith of corporate power, with its polished stone facade and the Fleetwood logo etched with a precision that suggested wealth was not just made here but orchestrated.

Inside, the vast lobby was designed to intimidate, with marble floors reflecting the harsh lighting above and chrome fixtures giving off a cold gleam. A receptionist sat behind a sleek desk, the only softness in this temple of commerce. She fidgeted with her pen, eyes darting between the two agents and the phone at her elbow as if expecting it to burst into flames.

"Can I help you?" Her voice trembled slightly, an off-note in the quietude.

"Special Agent Carly Phoenix, FBI. And this is Agent Grayson," Carly showed her badge. "We need to speak with someone from HR about an ongoing investigation."

"Uh—just a moment," stammered the receptionist, her fingers hesitating on the phone before she dialed. "Gina, we've got a problem. The FBI are here… I know… An agent Phoenix and Grayson."

Gina emerged like a wraith from the maze of cubicles beyond—a tall woman clad in a gray suit that seemed to swallow her small frame. Her hair was pulled back in a severe bun, and glasses perched precariously on her narrow nose. When Gray mentioned the homicides, the color drained from Gina's face, leaving her ashen under the unforgiving lights.

"Hello, I'm Gina Melnitz," she said, her confidence clearly only skin deep.

"As I was saying to your receptionist," Carly said. "We're here to investigate…"

"Please, follow me," Gina murmured, looking around nervously before leading them down a corridor lined with abstract art that looked more like investment than expression. Soon, they reached a gray door in an equally gray corridor and entered.

Gina's office was a cramped space, cluttered with files and personal touches attempting to claim some humanity amidst the corporate sterility. As they settled into chairs that felt too rigid for comfort, Carly couldn't ignore the hum of anxiety that seemed to vibrate through the walls.

"Everyone's on edge, Miss Melnitz," Carly observed, eyes locked onto Gina's. "Why?"

"Tomorrow could make or break us," Gina confessed, her hands clasped tightly on the desk. "Fleetwood is on the brink, and there's a buyout in play. If that meeting doesn't go well..."

"Bad timing for news of a double homicide to come up, wouldn't you say?" Gray chimed in, the hard lines of his face set in concern.

"Exactly." Gina's gaze flickered towards the door, as if the buyers might be eavesdropping. "The last thing we need is anything that comes close to a scandal."

Carly leaned back, taking in the fear that clung to Gina like a second skin. It wasn't just Fleetover's future that teetered on the edge—it was every person within these walls, their fates entwined with the company's survival. And yet, amid the impending chaos, Carly sensed opportunity—an opening that desperation might pry wide enough to slip through.

Carly fixed her gaze on Gina, the woman's face a mirror of worry and tight-lipped resistance. "Gina, I want to make it clear that we are not here to complicate your day any further," Carly said, her tone even but firm. "We're simply following a lead on a case—a double homicide from some years back. I'm sure it's nothing to worry about."

Gina's eyes darted between Carly and Gray, as if searching for something that might give her an out, but Carly's steady blue stare offered no such escape.

"Two women, Emily Rosario and Sarah Jennings," Carly continued, unblinking. "We have reason to believe they may have been at a fundraising event here in 1985 to raise donations for a place called Art déco."

Gray leaned forward, his voice cutting in with precision. "I know it was some time ago, but for tax purposes, I assume your company has kept such records in order to write off charitable donations and such. We'll need a list of attendees. If you kept records of events and guests, that would help us immensely."

Gina's already pale complexion seemed to drain of color at the mention of names and records. She looked from one agent to the other,

her mouth opening and then closing without a word.

"Anything you can provide would be helpful," Carly added, her words softening just enough to sound like she was offering Gina a lifeline rather than demanding evidence.

But Gina folded into herself, shoulders hunching as if bracing against a physical blow. "I can't," she murmured, her voice barely a whisper. "That was way before my time. Besides, it's confidential. Private company matters. And I certainly don't want to be exploring them on today of all days. There's so much to do."

"Even if it might help solve a murder?" Carly pressed, her patience fraying at the edges. She could sense Gray's disapproval at her prodding, the way he sat back ever so slightly in his chair.

"I'm sorry," Gina said, though her voice suggested that she was anything but.

"Imagine what would happen if the FBI had to escalate this situation," Carly said, the threat implicit in her words. "On the eve of your big takeover meeting, it would be unfortunate to have agents crawling over the place, wouldn't it?"

Gina bit her lip, visibly wrestling with the dilemma. Carly watched her closely, ready to pounce on the slightest crack in the HR manager's resolve.

After a long moment, Gina relented, asking, "When was the party?"

"Seventeenth of November," Carly replied, the date etched into her mind—the last night Emily Rosario was seen alive.

"1985," Gray added, just as Gina's fingers hovered over the keys of her computer, poised to unlock the past.

Carly watched Gina's fingers dance over the keyboard, a clacking rhythm like a train against the silence that filled the small office. The HR manager's eyes flickered across the screen, ticking off each record with an efficiency that belied the tension in her shoulders. Carly leaned forward, her anticipation sharpening the air around her as she waited for a breakthrough.

"Here," Gina said, breaking the silence. "The company holds meticulous records of all its events. There was indeed a fundraiser that night." A list of names cascaded down the monitor, a time-stamped testament to the past.

"Are the guests named?" Gray asked, his voice steady but insistent.

Gina paused, her eyes scanning the list. "Yes. It's all here."

"Can you print it out for us?" Carly interjected, her tone firm yet laced with an urgency that refused to be ignored.

Without another word, Gina hit the print command, and Carly

listened as the printer whirred to life, the sound like the beating wings of a moth trapped against a windowpane—desperate to escape. She watched as the paper gathered in the tray, each sheet heavy with potential clues, with voiceless faces from the past that might finally speak.

As Gina handed them the printout, Carly felt a surge of adrenaline. This list could hold the key to unlocking a door long sealed shut, a door behind which lay the monstrous truth of what happened to Emily Rosario and Sarah Jennings.

"Thank you for your help," Gray said, his voice reflecting both professionalism and relief.

"Of course," Gina replied, managing a tight smile. They left her there, amidst the starkness of her office, a lone figure in the looming shadow of corporate uncertainty.

Carly clutched the list close, feeling the weight of history in her hands. As they navigated through the maze of cubicles, she couldn't help but glance at the names, each one a potential lead. So engrossed was she in the sea of inked possibilities that she nearly collided with a group of suited men just outside the Fleetwood LTD entrance.

"Watch out," Gray murmured, tugging her back by the elbow. Her heart did a quickstep in her chest, but she steadied herself with a sheepish grin.

"Sorry," Carly offered to the businessmen, who were too preoccupied with their own concerns to pay her much mind. She and Gray shared a fleeting chuckle—that rare moment when the gravity of their work yielded to something lighter, something almost normal.

Stepping out of the building, Carly squinted against the glare of the setting sun reflecting off the Chicago skyline. She knew that they were walking away with more than just a list; they were carrying a fragile hope. The kind that had the power to bloom into answers or wilt into dead ends.

"Let's get back to the office and go over these names with a fine-toothed comb," Carly said, the excitement of the chase igniting once again within her. Gray nodded, his expression resolute.

*

The Chicago field office was a hive of activity as Carly and Gray returned with the list. They hunkered down in front of their computers in Gray's office, the air thick with the hum of hard drives and the soft click of keyboards. Carly's eyes darted across the screen as she input names from Fleetwood LTD's fundraiser guest list into the FBI database—a modern-day oracle that could either prophesy connections or cast doubts.

"Nothing," she said after a tense silence. "No criminal records, no warrants... it's like they're all angels."

"Clean slates don't always mean clean hands," Gray reminded her, his voice steady—like a lighthouse beam through fog.

"True." Carly leaned back, her mind racing through the shadows of possibility. Then something clicked: a detail about Emily Rosario that had been gnawing at her subconscious. "She was last seen getting into a truck..."

Gray looked up, a mixture of intrigue and caution in his gaze. Carly could almost see the gears turning behind his stoic facade.

"DMV records," she continued, "let's check if any of these guests had a CDL back then for trucking—or now."

"Good angle," he agreed and began to navigate through another set of databases, his fingers deftly moving across the keys. Time seemed to slow, each second stretching until...

"Got one," Gray announced, his tone lifting ever so slightly. "Benjamin Pierce, local truck driver. He's registered with…"

Carly leaned over to look at the screen. The name was like an ember that could start a wildfire, igniting a trail through years of cold evidence.

Gray leaned back for a moment, scratching his jaw in deep thought. "Let's find out who Benjamin Pierce really is," he finally said, reaching for his phone. Carly watched him dial with deliberate precision, the digits etching a path towards answers. He put the call on loudspeaker, and the ringing echoed briefly before a gruff voice answered.

"Daily Trucking, Dexter speaking."

"Michael Grayson, FBI. I'd like to talk about one of your drivers, Benjamin Pierce," Gray stated clearly, authority resonating in his tone.

"Ben? Sure, he's still with us. Been driving for ages," Dexter replied, a hint of confusion threading through his words.

"Was he working for you back in the '80s?" Gray pressed.

"Uh… I think so, he's one of the old timers, but we were under a different name then. Why? What's this about?"

"I assume your records go back some way. Can you provide details on his delivery routes for November 18th, 1985, and February 21st, 1986?" Gray's question hung in the air, weighty despite its simplicity.

"We might have it, but Look, I can't just hand out that kind of information. I'll need to clear it with my boss," Dexter cautioned.

"Understood," Gray replied, unyielding. "Please email the details to me."

"Alright, I'll see what I can do," Dexter conceded, albeit reluctantly.

The line went dead, and a heavy silence fell upon the room.

Carly's fingers stilled on the keyboard, her eyes fixed on the screen that had just gone dark with Dexter's final word. "We should hit the archives again," she said, pivoting in her chair to face Gray. "There could be something we missed, a detail that slipped through."

Gray was already standing, his gaze locked beyond the window where Chicago lay draped in the cloak of nightfall. The city's lights flickered like distant stars caught between silhouettes of towering structures—a metropolis holding its breath in the quiet before the storm.

"Carly," he started, turning back from the contemplation of the urban expanse. His voice carried the wisdom of countless nights spent chasing murderers down blind alleys. "We've been at this for hours. Our heads are spinning with information but no clarity. A fresh start in the morning might bring new perspective."

She considered arguing, her mind a relentless engine churning toward truth, but a yawn betrayed her fatigue. Carly rubbed at her eyes, the blue of them dimmed by exhaustion, and acknowledged the logic in his suggestion.

"Okay," she conceded, gathering her notes and shutting down her computer. "But first thing tomorrow, we pick up where we left off." Her voice held the determination of a woman who knew the value of persistence, who measured time not by the fall of dusk but by the closing of cases.

Gray nodded, and together they secured the office, the silence of their departure as poignant as the unanswered questions they left behind.

CHAPTER EIGHT

Night was falling fast, and Carly's breath misted the air as she strode briskly across the parking lot outside her apartment building, her footsteps dragging wearily on the asphalt. The cold bit at her cheeks, the kind of Chicago winter chill that seeped into your bones, uninvited and relentless. With each step closer to her apartment building, the shadows cast by the dim streetlights seemed to grow more pronounced, stretching out like dark fingers reaching for something just out of grasp.

Her mind, ever analytical, couldn't help but wander to Emily Rosario and Sarah Jennings. Their cases, their ends, haunted her—a hazy outline of violence that lingered in the night's frigid embrace. How had they felt in their final moments, wrapped not in the cold, but in the clutches of a predator? A shiver ran through Carly, not from the temperature, but from the eerie sense of vulnerability that clawed at her now, a feeling she detested.

The lobby was empty when she entered, but the security lights threw harsh angles across the tiled floor, painting a monochrome world that did little to ease the unease that had settled over her. She could almost feel the weight of unseen eyes tracking her progress, spiking her stress levels—whether from fear or the remnants of adrenaline from the day's revelations, she couldn't be certain.

As Carly approached her door, the silence felt oppressive, a quiet so dense it seemed to muffle the sound of her own footsteps. It was in this stillness that she sensed it—the subtle shift in the air, an instinct honed by years of hunting the hunted. Someone was there, behind her, close enough to share the same whispered breath of the hallway.

She turned abruptly, her hand instinctively reaching toward the firearm that sat snugly in its holster, expecting to find some creep stalking her every move.

Instead, she found herself face-to-face with a man who appeared as if conjured from the shadows themselves. He stood tall, black hair falling just shy of his eyes, which held a spark of youth that suggested he was in his late twenties or early thirties. His attractiveness was offset by the disheveled state of his clothing, overalls splattered with paint that told a story of a different day's work.

"Hello there," he said, with a voice smooth like worn leather, yet edged with the roughness of someone who made their living by the sweat of their brow rather than the turn of a phrase. His presence caught her off guard—not threatening, but unexpected. Too unexpected. Carly's blue gaze raked over him once more, searching for any sign that he might not be what he seemed, a habit ingrained in her very marrow.

"Hi," Carly responded, her tone even, but her stance poised and ready. Her FBI training never really left her, and neither did the caution that came with it. This man, smeared with the evidence of his trade, was an unknown quantity. And Carly didn't like unknowns.

Her breath steadied as she watched the man extend a hand, his smile disarmingly boyish beneath the streaks of white and cobalt that adorned his cheek. "Hemingway," he said, with an ease that seemed to cut through the tension that had seized her moments before. "That's my name."

"Like the writer?" Carly replied, her mind still ticking over the possibilities of this late-night encounter, talents honed from years in the Behavioral Analysis Unit unwilling to fully disengage.

"Exactly," Hemingway smirked, ruffling his hair, causing a small shower of dried paint flecks to cascade down. "Parents had high hopes, I guess. Earned me a lot of book-themed beatings in school."

He didn't seem to want sympathy; the joke was as much a shield as it was a bridge. Carly noted the deflection but played along. "I'm Carly, I just moved in. You look more like a painter than a writer."

"That's because I am, at the moment." He gestured to his overalls, where colors warred in silent battles across the fabric. "Just working on my place. I saw you standing in the hallway and wanted to say hello, welcome you to the building. I'm just a couple of doors down from you. Speaking of which, I was about to head out to my car and get another set of brushes from my trunk."

"It's a cold one out there and I could barely get a space," Carly said, her words carrying the shared camaraderie of fellow city-dwellers battling for coveted street space.

"Tell me about it," Hemingway agreed, his smile easy but his eyes scanning the hallway, perhaps already plotting his strategy. "Holler if you ever need anything." He smiled and turned to leave.

Carly reached for her apartment key, the metal felt cold and unyielding in her grip. She put it in the lock and found that it stuck. Jiggling it around, she ended up in a tired fight with the door, and she was losing. She started to think it was the wrong key.

Hemingway laughed from the end of the hallway and walked over, leaned in, his proximity a sudden heat in the chill of the corridor. "Those locks can be tricky," he said, his tone suggesting familiarity rather than presumption. "Mine sticks sometimes. You've got to give it a whack."

She hesitated, a flicker of reluctance crossing her features, but something about Hemingway's earnestness nudged her to acquiesce, there was something homely about him, like a boy raised on a picturesque farm. He tapped the key just so, and the tumblers yielded, the door swinging open with a soft creak that spoke of long nights and lonely returns in the future.

"Thanks," Carly murmured, but her gratitude faltered as she caught sight of a fresh splotch of paint marring the wood of her door—a casualty of Hemingway's earlier artistic endeavors.

"Ah, crap," Hemingway muttered, his handsome face crumpling into an expression of genuine dismay. Clumsily, he pulled a rag from his pocket, dabbing at the offending mark. Instead of diminishing, the smudge grew, a stubborn stain spreading its territory.

"Here, let me—" Carly started, but Hemingway's hands were already fumbling, the rag more an instrument of chaos than cleaning.

"Sorry, I'm usually not this..." He trailed off, the word 'disastrous' hanging unspoken between them. His mortification was a palpable thing, filling the space with an awkward energy that made Carly's skin prickle—not with danger, but with empathy.

"Hey, it's okay," Carly assured him, though part of her—a part trained to scrutinize and suspect—wondered if there was more to this clumsy neighbor than met the eye.

"I am so sorry about this."

Carly's gaze didn't waver as she studied the man before her, his eyes wide with a mix of embarrassment and something that might have been anxiety.

"You know," she said, voice steady, "I'm an FBI agent, and technically, this is vandalism." The words hung in the air between them, charged with an authority that Carly wielded with ease—even if she were only joking this time.

Hemingway's face drained of color, and he stumbled over his words, a flustered stammer that clashed with the easy charm he had exuded moments ago. "I-I'm so sorry, I didn't mean to—"

But Carly couldn't keep up the charade. She let out a laugh, loud and genuine, breaking the tension like a pin to a balloon. "Relax, Hemingway, I'm just messing with you." She nudged the door wider with her foot, leaning against the frame. "But you do realize you're going to have to paint the rest now, right?" The amusement in her eyes was clear, even as they flicked toward the smeared paint, assessing.

"Ugh, with pleasure, Ma'am," Hemingway replied, recovering his composure with a sheepish grin.

"Ma'am makes me feel old, Carly will do," she smiled.

He stood straighter, the rag hanging limp in his hand. "By the way, I'm in number 305." He gestured vaguely down the hallway, where other doors stood silent sentinels to the lives within. "If you ever need anything—cup of coffee, or... anything."

"Thanks," Carly acknowledged, nodding. There was something oddly comforting about the mundane offer, a normalcy that her life often lacked. "But let's just start with painting over my door."

"Agreed. Good night then," he said, turning away with a wave. But as he reached the end of the corridor, he must have touched the door to the stairwell, leaving yet a smudge of paint on yet another door, mirroring his earlier accident at Carly's. "Oh man," he groaned, half-laughing, half-resigned. "I'm going to be painting the whole building at this rate."

The corner of Carly's mouth twitched upward as she watched him go, his figure retreating into the quietude of the corridor. She pushed her door open wider, stepping into the sanctuary of her own space, the echo of Hemingway's self-deprecating humor lingering like the faint scent of fresh paint.

Carly's smile trailed off as she slipped through the doorway, feeling the solid click of the door shutting behind her like a line drawn between the world outside and her own private sanctuary. She was home, and with that thought, the weight of the day's gravity seemed to intensify, pressing upon her shoulders with a silent insistence. The apartment was dark; the only light spilling in from the streetlamps outside cut across the floor in slivers through the blinds, partitioning the room into uneven segments of shadow and amber glow.

As she moved through the quiet, Carly's fingers found the wall switch, and the kitchen was bathed in a sterile fluorescence that seemed too harsh for the hour. On the counter lay her address book, its pages splayed open, revealing scrawled names and numbers like a directory of her past. One name stood out, emboldened by its significance: "Justin"—a name that held histories and heartaches, memories she could not afford to unpack at this hour.

When their mother had died, Carly had done her best to look out for him. It was her duty as his big sister, but eventually, it all crumbled to dust. Carly left Chicago behind after that, a place she thought she was done with, but now she was back. The pain of confronting that was too much at times. Instead, she kept a wall up to stop her world from imploding. That was the way it was with Carly. Pain had to be ringfenced, hidden away forever. The problem was, it wasn't forever, and Carly knew that deep down. Any pain bad enough like that, filled with regret and family burden, would always claw its way up from the grave.

Shaking her head, Carly touched her fingertips to the page as if she could smooth away the complexities of her relationship with her brother as easily as creases in paper. "Later," she whispered to the empty room, the words a promise or a prevarication, even she wasn't sure.

Her legs felt heavy as she shuffled towards the bedroom, each step an echo in the stillness. She didn't bother with the lights; the dark shapes of furniture guided her. The bed loomed, a monolith of solace in the dimness. With movements devoid of grace, Carly let herself fall onto it, the mattress accepting her form with a gentle creak.

The ceiling above offered no answers, only the faint, cobwebbed contours of a life lived in pursuit and penance. Her eyelids grew heavy with the effort of keeping the day at bay, and she surrendered to the encroaching tide of exhaustion. Tomorrow would come with its demands and its questions, but for now, she allowed the silence to claim her, the last vestiges of consciousness slipping away like owls at dawn.

CHAPTER NINE

The shrill ring of the phone shattered Carly's dreams like a sledgehammer through glass. She groped blindly for the device, eyes still gummed with sleep, and brought it to her ear. The voice on the other end was immediate and unyielding, slicing through the fog in her mind.

"Phoenix, we have something. The trucking company sent over Pierce's routes from '85 and '86, first thing." Gray's words were brisk, efficient.

Carly squinted at the luminous numbers on her digital clock: 6:30 AM. Her body protested the early hour as she sat up, rubbing the sleep from her eyes. "Do you ever sleep, Gray?"

"Sleep is for the dead," he retorted, a hint of dark humor in his otherwise stoic tone.

"I'll be at the office in an hour," she replied, swinging her legs off the bed, her hair resting over her shoulders, messily.

"No need. I'm sending you the address for Daily Trucking. Pierce is on-site today, we should corner him."

"Got it." Carly ended the call, her mind already racing with possibilities. As she pulled herself out of bed, determination etched into every line of her lean frame, the sense of purpose that always came with the chase began to dispel the last remnants of sleep.

*

The Chicago morning air bit at Carly's skin as she stepped out of her car, a paper cup of steaming coffee clutched in one hand. The sprawling expanse of Daily Trucking loomed before her, its industrial facade grim and sharp against the soft light of dawn. She found Gray waiting, his gray hair tousled by the wind, his posture rigid with anticipation. She wondered what age he was, forties, she guessed, as the remnants of youth could still be seen on display.

"Tell me you brought a second cup," Gray said, eyeing the coffee.

"Sorry, completely slipped my mind," Carly apologized, feeling a twinge of regret for the minor oversight.

A smile briefly cut through Gray's seriousness. "Relax, Phoenix. I'm capable of cracking a joke or two."

It was a rare glimpse into the softer side of Michael Grayson, a man who wore his years of service like armor. Carly took a sip of her coffee, letting the warmth and bitterness ground her thoughts.

"Ready?" she asked.

"It would be rude not to," he replied, and together they approached the depot, hoping to find evidence of a long-forgotten killer.

Gray pulled out something from his inside pocket as they walked.

Carly caught the paper as Gray flipped it her way, the map snapping under its own weight as it unfurled. The inked lines were a spider's web of possible guilt, routes that crisscrossed and skirted the edges of infamy. She traced the path with her finger, the coffee's steam curling up between them like an invisible barrier. They showed two truck routes, each dated the same nights as Emily Rosario and Sarah Jennings were killed.

"Less than half a mile from each," she murmured, the numbers and facts aligning with cold precision in her mind. "He was right there. Both times. It's got to be him."

"Coincidences don't hold up in a court of law, Phoenix," Gray said, his voice tinged with the edge of a man who had seen too many coincidences to believe in them. "Let's see where we get. Our point of contact should be a guy called Marshall, the admin worker I spoke to this morning said he was in charge of the shop today."

The depot door loomed before them, a portal to answers they might not be ready to hear. With a shared glance, they stepped into the cavernous interior, the scent of oil and metal anointing their entrance.

Inside, the workshop spread out like a graveyard of mechanical beasts, trucks in states of disrepair baring their innards to the world. Grease-stained hands worked diligently, accompanied by a series of clinks, clangs, and hisses that spoke of life amidst the decay.

"Marshall?" Carly called out, her badge held aloft like a shield. A man surfaced from under the hood of an engine, wiping his hands on a rag as if to clean away culpability along with the grime, his bald head catching the light from above. His eyes were wide with annoyance.

"Can I help you? We're very busy today," he said, wiping grease from his hands.

"We're from the FBI," Carly said. "We'd appreciate your assistance."

"Do you have someone working here today named Benjamin

Pierce?" Gray added, his tone suggesting this was no friendly chat.

Marshall's eyes darted around, seeking invisible exits. "Look, I don't want any trouble..."

"Trouble finds us all, Marshall," Carly interjected, her gaze steady. "But you can choose what side of it you're on."

"If this is an issue with the law," Marshall continued. "I'm staying out of it. If this Pierce guy is around, you'll need to find him yourself." He moved as if to turn his back and walk over to the truck he was working on.

Gray leaned in, his hair catching the light from above. "How does 'accessory to murder' sound for size?"

The color drained from Marshall's face faster than oil from a busted pan. He jerked his thumb towards the behemoth trucks, where a red cap bobbed between chrome and steel.

"Benjamin Pierce," he said, his voice barely above a whisper, pointing them towards a large red truck hoisted on hydraulics.

They walked towards where Marshall had pointed, and turned around the side of a large red truck suspended by hydraulics, several men busying themselves around it.

Most of them were too young, so Carly approached the oldest looking, a man in a red cap with a cautious stride, her eyes tracing the lines of age that etched his face. He looked up from his work, his gaze wary but not alarmed, as if interrupted thoughts were a common occurrence in the hum of the workshop.

"Benjamin Pierce?" Carly's voice cut through the air, clear and authoritative.

He nodded, an almost imperceptible lift of his chin that told her he was accustomed to being sought after, but not necessarily for conversations he'd welcome.

"Special Agent Carly Phoenix," she continued, flashing her badge briefly. "We need to talk."

Some of the men gave Benjamin a worried look. His eyes narrowed in response, assessing, then he gestured to a door that led away from the clamor of the garage. As they walked, Carly noted how his steps were measured, how he carried himself with a quiet confidence that contradicted the disarray of his work environment.

The room they entered was spare, insulated from the noise outside. It felt like stepping into a vacuum, where sounds were swallowed whole and secrets lingered in the corners. Carly took a breath as they sat down, feeling the shift in dynamic as they faced each other across a battered metal table.

“Where were you on the 17th of November, 1985, and February 21st, 1986?” Gray asked, his voice steady but heavy with implication.

Pierce’s brow furrowed, his shock genuine—or a masterful imitation. “That’s a helluva long time ago. What’s this about?”

“Two murders,” Carly said, watching his reaction closely. His features tensed, then relaxed into an expression of disbelief.

“Murders?” Pierce echoed, the word hanging between them like a verdict waiting to be delivered.

Carly was unnerved by the incongruity of it all. She had expected evasion, nervousness, perhaps anger. Not this serene acceptance.

“Try to remember,” Gray insisted. “These dates are important.”

“Yes,” Carly pressed on, leaning forward. “One in late 1985, the other in late 1986. Your routes put you within striking distance of both crime scenes at that time. What can you tell us about those nights?”

His laughter was unexpected, a low rumble that seemed out of place in the sterile room. “Agent, I’ve driven so many miles these years, nights blend into days, dates into seasons.” But his calm demeanor didn’t waver, and Carly’s intuition prickled in return.

Pierce leaned back in his chair, fingers drumming a silent rhythm on the tabletop. “I might have been out there,” he conceded slowly, “but I wasn’t involved in any murders.”

“Can anyone vouch for your whereabouts?” Carly asked, her stare locked onto his, searching for the fractures in his story.

He met her stare unflinchingly. “I keep to myself mostly,” he replied. “But I’m telling you, you’ve got the wrong guy.”

“Being near the scene of a crime once could be coincidence,” Carly reasoned, her mind racing through possible scenarios. “Twice is a pattern. We need more than your word, Mr. Pierce.”

Pierce shook his head, a trace of weariness creeping into his posture. “You won’t find what you’re looking for here,” he said, his tone even but firm.

“Then help us understand,” Gray urged. “How do we cross you off our list of suspects?”

For a moment, Carly thought she saw something flicker behind Pierce’s eyes—a hint of fear at the thought of being led away in cuffs in front of his co-workers.

"Fine," Pierce relented. "I'll need to see the routes you're talking about and the specific dates."

Gray handed the printout to him.

Carly watched the man across from her unfold the map with a casualness that seemed out of place in the cramped break room of Daily

Trucking. Benjamin Pierce's hands, though marked by years on the road, moved with a precision younger than his years. As he traced the lines that crisscrossed the city, his eyes flickered with recognition—then amusement.

He laughed again.

"See this?" Pierce pointed to a number imprinted next to the route for February 21st, 1986.

"That's truck 17-B. I was driving 17-A that night. The company reused the numbers after decommissioning the old models. Simple admin error. That second route isn't me. And I can prove it."

Gray leaned forward, the skepticism etched into his weathered face softening. "You're saying you have an alibi for both dates?"

"Absolutely." Pierce said. "I fancied myself as an engineer back then, though it didn't pan out. I was flunking thermodynamics at Glorfid Community College when your first victim bit the dust. I wasn't even in the state in February of 1986."

"We'll check with the college… Still," Gray persisted, "you were close to the first scene the night Emily Rosario was murdered."

"Half a mile close," Pierce chuckled without humor, leaning back in his chair. "But so were hundreds of others. That stretch by the lake? It's a main artery. You're looking for a needle in a haystack. Most truckers in Chicago use it for long hauls out of the city."

The words hung heavy in the air between them. Carly felt the edges of the mystery fray further as she folded the map, placing it inside her coat. She locked eyes with Pierce one last time, searching for something—anything—that might betray his calm demeanor.

But all she saw was a man trying to do his job.

"Thanks for your cooperation," she offered, but her words were hollow, echoing off the walls of dead ends they now faced.

"We'll be in touch if that alibi doesn't pan out," Gray said, before following Carly back into the shop and then into the frozen morning.

Outside, the cold Chicago wind bit through Carly's jacket as she walked alongside Gray to their respective cars. Daily Trucking loomed behind them, a monolith of metal and concrete that now felt meaningless in their search.

"If his story checks out," Gray said, breaking the silence. "We'll confirm with the college, but..."

"It looks like he's just some random guy," Carly interjected, her gaze still fixed on the building's façade. "But we can't rule him out completely. I wonder if we should watch him and see if he goes anywhere under pressure."

"Be careful you don't see ghosts because you want to," Gray countered, his voice tinged with the weariness that came with too many years chasing shadows. "Cold cases will do that to you. Make you chase phantoms. This is likely nothing. I'll see you back at the office."

"Bye."

Carly slid into her car, the leather seat cold against her skin. She watched Gray walk away, his gait steady and sure. He seemed undaunted by hitting a wall, but jaded too, as though he accepted it all too quickly.

"Dammit," she whispered, her breath fogging up the windshield. She turned the key in the ignition, the engine's growl a reluctant admission of their impasse.

CHAPTER TEN

February, 1987…

Hannah Grimes' breath formed frozen wisps as she stepped through the sliding doors of the bar, a far cry from the sterilized halls of the hospital where she'd spent her night shift. The neon sign above flickered half-heartedly, casting an eerie glow on the freshly fallen snow that blanketed Chicago's streets like a shroud. It was the kind of winter that gnawed at the bones, the kind that made the cityscape seem more desolate, more unforgiving.

Inside, the warmth of the Oval Portrait hit Hannah like a soothing balm. She peeled off her thick scarf, revealing curly blonde hair that immediately frizzed from the temperature change. Her green eyes, usually bright with the compassion she afforded her patients, now held a glint of weary relief as she settled into the corner booth that had become her refuge after these brutal nights.

The bar was dimly lit, each table haloed by the soft glow of overhead lamps. Laughter and conversation hummed around her, a comforting reminder of life outside the hospital walls. With practiced motions, she shrugged out of her overcoat and smoothed the fabric of her uniform before signaling the bartender.

"Whiskey sour, please," Hannah said, her voice betraying the hint of a smile. It was her small act of rebellion against the cold, a ritual to warm her up from the inside out. The bartender nodded, familiar with the routine, and soon slid the drink across the polished wood countertop towards her.

She cupped the glass in her hands, savoring the heat that seeped into her skin. It was moments like these—quiet, solitary—that allowed her to transition from nurse to just Hannah. The Hannah who loved mystery novels, who had recently fallen hard for a man whose name she dared not speak aloud for fear it might break the spell.

As she took a sip, the sharp tang of citrus mingled with the smooth burn of whiskey. She let the flavors linger, closing her eyes briefly. In her mind's eye, she could see her lover's face, the curve of his smile, the way his laughter seemed to resonate deep within her chest. It was a dangerous thing, this love; it crept up on her stealthily, with the silent determination of the winter's first frost.

Hannah opened her eyes again, grounding herself in the present. The condensation from her drink left her fingertips damp, and she drew patterns on the wooden table absentmindedly. She knew that outside, the city was harsh, unrelenting, but here, in her corner booth with a drink in hand, the world seemed just a little kinder, a little less bleak.

And yet, even surrounded by the low murmur of conversation and the occasional clink of glassware, there was a palpable tension in the air, an undercurrent of something she couldn't quite place. It niggled at the back of her mind, a whisper of unease that she quickly tried to dismiss. After all, this was her time, her moment of reprieve.

"Another cold one," she murmured to herself, watching as a couple laughed at a nearby table. Their joy was infectious, and for a fleeting second, Hannah allowed herself the luxury of imagining a different life—one filled with normalcy, with the promise of shared warmth against the chill of another Chicago winter.

But the reality was that she was here, alone with her thoughts and the remnants of her drink, the shadows playing tricks on her senses. And though she couldn't shake the feeling that something was amiss, Hannah Grimes, compassionate and steadfast, would continue to seek solace in these small moments of peace amidst the chaos of her calling.

The bar's warmth was a far cry from the icy chill that had settled over Chicago streets. Hannah Grimes, nestled in the corner with her coat still buttoned against the possibility of a draft, scanned the half-empty glasses on her table—a record of time spent unwinding after her shift. Her fingers pressed against the fabric of her scrubs, the texture grounding her, reminding her of the lives she'd touched just hours before.

A man slid onto the seat beside her with an ease that contradicted the staccato rhythm of the jazz band playing in the background. A waft of his cologne, something woodsy and comforting, cut through the smoky haze of the bar. She caught the flicker of curiosity in his eyes as he turned to her, a smile playing at the edges of his lips.

"Mind if I sit here?" His voice was smooth, almost melodic, and it pulled her from her reverie with the gentleness of a practiced hand.

"Go ahead," Hannah replied, shifting to acknowledge him, her own smile cautious but genuine.

"I couldn't help but notice you're wearing scrubs," he said, gesturing toward her attire with an artist's attention to detail. "A nurse?"

She nodded, taken aback by the observance. “Yeah, just off a late shift.”

“Ah, then you must be an angel in disguise.” His grin widened, revealing a set of well-maintained teeth. “I’m an artist myself. I try to capture the essence of those who give so much of themselves to others.”

“An artist, huh?” Hannah’s eyebrows rose, both skeptical and intrigued. “What do you paint?”

“Mostly life’s candid moments—the ones that tell stories without words.” He leaned in slightly, conspiratorial. “And sometimes, the darker edges of those stories.”

Hannah considered him for a moment, his hands—long-fingered and seemingly adept at holding brushes—resting casually on the bar. There was something magnetic about him, yet she couldn’t shake a flicker of caution that whispered beneath the surface of their conversation.

“Sounds... interesting.” The ambiguity of her response was intentional; a way to keep the door open while guarding the threshold.

Time passed quickly, and as they talked, Hannah found herself losing her gaze in his. By the fourth drink, she decided that she should leave the bar, otherwise she might end up powerless against his charms.

“It’s been lovely,” she said. “But I really have to go. I have a shift at the hospital in the morning.”

“Of course,” he said, glancing toward the window where frost etched crooked patterns on the glass, “it’s treacherous out there tonight. Would you allow me the honor of walking you home? It’s no weather for anyone to face alone.”

A nurse’s instinct for assessing situations kicked in, measuring the sincerity in his offer against the practicality of venturing into the winter’s night solo. Hannah weighed her options, the allure of safety in numbers against the silent alarms that refused to quiet down entirely.

“Alright,” she said finally, a decision made more out of necessity than desire, her voice betraying none of the hesitation that pinched at the corners of her mind. “Thank you, that’s very kind.”

“Kindness is easy in the company of someone dedicated to healing others,” he replied, his tone light, as though they were merely two souls crossing paths in the vast tapestry of the city’s nightlife.

Hannah finished her drink, the liquid courage not quite reaching the tendrils of doubt that danced around her thoughts. She slipped off the stool, aware of the weight of his gaze upon her as she buttoned her coat, pulling the fabric close as if it could shield her from more than just the cold.

They stepped into the biting air outside, the shift from the bar's warmth to Chicago's wintry embrace immediate and unforgiving. The young man—artist or not—followed suit, his posture relaxed as he pushed the door closed behind them. The laughter and clinking of glasses faded into a muffled backdrop against the howl of the wind.

"Brutal, isn't it?" he said, his breath a cloud of vapor in the frigid night. He tucked his hands into the pockets of his pea coat, the heavy fabric seeming to shield him adequately from the elements.

"Nothing I'm not used to," Hannah replied, her words edged with the chill that crept through her layers. She glanced up and down the street, comforted by the occasional passerby hurrying to their own destinations. The presence of others—strangers all the same—provided a thin veil of safety. It was enough to keep her company on this short journey.

"Still, one can never be too cautious," he remarked, his mouth lifting in a kind smile, though his eyes were shaded by the dim streetlights, unreadable.

"Especially on nights like this." Hannah caught herself talking more to affirm her own security than to continue the conversation. They began walking, footsteps crunching on the snow-packed sidewalk.

As they progressed, the bustling noise of city life receded, leaving them enveloped in a strange, quiet cocoon. The wind seemed to whisper secrets as it danced through barren branches overhead. Streetlights flickered intermittently, casting long, wavering shadows that merged with the darkness between their pools of light. The surrounding buildings stood silent, windows darkened, doors tightly shut against the winter assault. The neighborhood had taken on an eerie stillness, and the faint sense of camaraderie from the bar now seemed worlds away.

Hannah wrapped her arms around herself, the initial assurance of being accompanied starting to wane. Her heart thudded a little harder, its rhythm incongruent with the calm she tried to exude.

"Are we close to where you live?" the man said, his voice a soft intrusion into the growing unease that buzzed at the edge of Hannah's senses. It should have been a reassurance, but instead it hung in the air—a promise or perhaps a prelude.

"Yes," Hannah murmured, her gait steady despite the uncertainty that nipped at her heels. There was nothing tangible to name, no concrete reason to distrust the man by her side, yet the night itself seemed to hold its breath, waiting for something to shatter the silence.

Hannah's breath unfurled in a silvery cloud that dissipated into the night as she quickened her pace. The city sounds had dulled to a hush, muffled by the thick snow that blanketed Chicago's streets. Her companion's footsteps fell in sync with hers, a metronome to her racing heart. She could feel the cold seeping through the soles of her shoes, numbing her toes.

She stopped at a dimly lit street corner and looked the man in his eyes. There was something about them now, like the warmth back at the bar had been replaced by a terrible coldness.

Although it was a lie, she thought it best to part from him.

"I'm just up this street. Thank you for walking me home," Hannah said, her voice steady though a tremor of unease quivered through her. It was just the winter chill, she assured herself, not the proximity of this stranger, this artist who had appeared out of the blue.

"Of course," he replied, his tone smooth like the surface of the ice that glazed the sidewalks. "But let me escort you a little further. I wouldn't want you to face this cold alone."

He slipped his arm around her and began walking with more force up the street. Hannah was in a daze and didn't know whether to scream or just hope he would let her go when she lied about one of the apartment buildings being her own.

The lampposts cast an amber glow, but between them shadows stretched across their path, as if reaching for something just out of grasp. With each step, the night seemed to grow denser, its weariness more palpable. Hannah couldn't shake the creeping feeling that with every echo of their footfalls, something was being left behind. Something intangible, like the final notes of a song hanging in the air before fading to silence.

She reached up, her fingers reaching the soft wool of her scarf—a gift from a man whose name she cherished within the quiet confines of her heart. Pulling the fabric closer around her neck, she secured it tightly, a barrier against the biting wind and the unnamed dread that slithered along her spine. The scarf smelled faintly of antiseptic, a stark reminder of her world of white linens and whispered comforts, so far removed from the dark, sleeping city around her.

Hannah pointed to one of the buildings.

"Here we are," the stranger said, gesturing to the same old brick building that loomed ahead, its windows dark, save for one that flickered weakly in a distant apartment.

"Right," Hannah replied, her gaze flitting to the rectangle of light that promised warmth and solitude. But her hand remained clutched at her scarf, knuckles pale, as if the simple act of holding on could ground her in a reality that suddenly felt as frigid and fragile as the ice underfoot.

"Goodnight then," he said, the words almost a whisper, but there was no response from Hannah. She merely nodded, the motion stiff and automatic, as she turned toward the safety of her building.

Something wrapped around her throat from behind. She tried to scream, tried to fight, but quickly, she felt herself losing consciousness, her milky white hands grasping at cold air. She closed her eyes as she thought, dragged into a doorway nearby, leaving the night to swallow the space where she'd been, as though she'd never been there at all.

CHAPTER ELEVEN

Present Day.

Carly leaned back against her desk, the stark chill of the dossier's metal clasp pressing into her palm as she flipped it open. The record player in Gray's corner of the office spilled out the strains of a classical piece, the violins sawing in a haunting melody that seemed to seep into the very walls of the room. She watched Gray for a moment, wearing smart, black-rimmed glasses she hadn't seen before, his jaw working furiously on a piece of gum, his gaze lost in thought.

"What's with the gum?" Carly asked, the question breaking the silence like a pinprick to the bubble of concentration.

Gray glanced up, a flicker of annoyance crossing his features before he composed himself. "Helps me think," he grumbled, pushing the wad around with his tongue. "Though I wish it were a cigar. Like the old days."

"Smoke-filled rooms and trench coats, huh?" Carly quipped, a half-smile tugging at her lips. "If it were a cigar, I might've joined you. For the ambiance."

Gray snorted, a semblance of a smile softening the hard lines around his eyes. He shifted in his seat, turning slightly toward her. "How are you finding Chicago?"

The question was casual, but Carly felt the weight of her past press against her chest. She had spent parts of her childhood here, but those memories were still wrapped in shadows, the edges too raw to touch. "I like it," she lied smoothly, evading the inquiry.

Her attention returned to the file in front of her, her thumb running over the frayed edge of the folder as she sifted through the papers. Then she stopped cold. A police report, its edges yellowed with age, detailed the murder of Hannah Grimes. Two details leaped from the page: the date, February 3rd, 1987, and the location where her body was found—on the edge of a line of trees. Just like Emily and Sarah.

"Another winter stabbing," Carly murmured, but her anticipation of a breakthrough increasing. She turned to Gray, the file now splayed open like an accusation on her desk. "And another body by a treeline."

Gray's chair creaked as he leaned forward, his expression tightening. "What do you have?"

"Look at this." She gestured to the file, tapping on the date, then the description of the crime scene. "It's too similar to be a coincidence."

Gray pulled off his glasses, rubbing the bridge of his nose. Carly could see the gears turning in his head, the procedural machine whirring to life behind his analytical eyes. He replaced his glasses, meeting Carly's gaze squarely. "You might be onto something, it is very similar, thought not exact. We've got to tread carefully. Patterns like these... they can mislead."

"Or lead us right to the killer," Carly countered, filled with the thrill of the chase.

"You also have to remember," Gray explained, "that the families of the dead are still waiting for answers all these years later. We don't want to give them hope that the investigation is truly alive again until we're certain we're on the right track."

The record player crackled, the music reaching swelling before tapering into silence

Carly moved over to Grays desk and said: "Hannah Grimes, that was the name."

Her gaze lingered on Gray's computer screen as he perused a sea of digital case files. The click-clack of his keyboard was like rain, a backdrop to the whir of thoughts in her head.

"There," he said, his voice snapping her to attention. "Hannah Grimes' case file."

"Got anything more on her than is in here?" Carly asked, leaning closer. Her eyes darted across the screen, seeking patterns in the pixels.

"She was a nurse," Gray replied, scrolling through the information. "32 years old. Worked at St. Agnes Hospital for nearly a decade."

"Stabbed and left at a treeline," Carly pondered aloud. It sounded like a broken record, the same grim tune repeating itself. "Do you think she could be our third?"

Gray's jaw tightened, and Carly knew that caution was his creed. "Could be random," he mused. "But your insight hasn't steered us wrong yet."

"Then let's check out where she was found," Carly suggested, already rising from her seat. "We need to see it for ourselves."

Gray nodded, and together they grabbed their coats, quickly heading out of the building and stepping into the raw bite of a Chicago winter. Carly's breath fogged before her as they made their way to the unmarked sedan. The cold had a cleansing edge to it, stripping away all but the most persistent of thoughts. And Carly's were persistent indeed.

*

The line of trees stood sentry on the outskirts of Chicago, barren branches clawing at an overcast sky. Carly and Gray's footsteps crunched in the snow as they traced the perimeter where Hannah Grimes' life had ended so abruptly.

"Here." Carly stopped, pulling out glossy photographs from a manila folder. She held them up to the treeline, comparing angles, looking for parallels in the daylight. "The similarities are striking."

"Indeed," Gray acknowledged, his eyes tracing the lines of trunks and shadows. "If this was him, the killer has a preference for these natural backdrops. A signature of sorts."

"A fingerprint of its own," Carly suggested. Her mind raced with the possibilities.

Each tree felt like a silent witness, its secrets locked behind layers of bark and time. She imagined Hannah Grimes' final moments, the stark horror of death meeting the quiet world of these woods. It made her feel sick to her stomach.

"Let's walk it again," Carly said, determination sharpening her features. She moved methodically, Gray a steady presence by her side. They were a study in contrasts—her impulsive energy against his measured calm—but united in purpose.

The scene was empty now, save for their own footprints marring the perfection of the snow. Carly's breath misted in the cold air as she stood, her gaze drawn to the rhythm of life pulsing from a nearby train station beyond the patch of woods. Commuters, bundled against Chicago's unforgiving winter, flowed in a steady stream in the distance, their footsteps echoing the dull thrum of urgency that seemed to reverberate through the city's infrastructure. Her fingers tightened around the worn edges of the crime scene photos as she turned back to Gray.

"Only five," she mused aloud, more to herself than Gray, her eyes narrowing. "Hannah was stabbed five times, not thirteen like Emily and Sarah."

"An inconsistency," Gray replied, his voice carrying the weight of skepticism. "Could be a different killer. Could be random."

"Or..." Carly hesitated, then pointed towards the train station, its lights a beacon of civilization amidst the desolation. "The killer might have been interrupted. People leaving the station up ahead, catching him in the act. It's far enough away for him to think this place was secluded, but close enough for someone to wander this way and see him."

Gray chewed his gum slower, considering her words. "There's no mention of a witness in the case files." His statement dangled between them, heavy with unspoken doubt.

"You know you're outside now," Carly said. "You could smoke a cigar if you wanted, too."

"I'm trying to quit," Gray said. "It would be handy if there had been a witness. But we have to assume no one contacted the police."

"Doesn't mean there wasn't a witness." Carly's eyes were steely, her mind weaving through the tapestry of what-ifs. "Witnesses don't always come forward. Fear, guilt... or maybe they just didn't realize what they saw."

He looked at her, a hint of admiration breaking through his stoic demeanor. "I like the way you think, Phoenix. You use informed speculation well, but we need substance, evidence, if we're to link Hannah's death to Emily's and Sarah's."

She gave him a tight-lipped smile, respecting his caution but unwilling to temper her own tenacity. They were hunting a phantom stitched together from years of silence and overlooked details. She wouldn't let caution blind them to potential revelations. She was getting into the mentality of a cold case investigator already. And she like to kick up the dust to see what it revealed.

"We have a victim who was left in a similar way, but a different number of stab wounds, and there is no wide open space like Lake Michigan opposite the treeline. There is only a small space then the clearing over there, which would count against your theory that the killer, if it is the same man, is recreating a scene or image… Unless… Wait," Gray said suddenly, his focus shifting.

Carly watched him closely, noting the change in his posture, the intentness that sharpened his features. "What is it?"

"Over there." He gestured towards another treeline opposite where they had been examining the crime scene. She followed without question, trusting his experience as they carved a path through the underbrush and then moved into the woodland opposite, weaving between the trees.

They emerged into a clearing, an unexpected fracture from the past unveiled before them—an old outdoor amphitheater, its grandeur succumbed to decay. Nature had staked its claim, trees sprouting with wild abandon through the cracked stone steps, a monument to abandonment.

"Forty years ago," Gray murmured, almost to himself, "this place would have been alive with applause. An artist's haven."

Carly stepped carefully over the encroaching roots, her mind casting back to an era when the amphitheater played host to eager audiences. "An artist," she echoed thoughtfully, a new piece of the puzzle slotting into place. "You're suggesting this could be about performance? About being seen? He killed in front of the amphitheater, which would have been empty at night, imagining his adoring audience?"

"Perhaps," Gray conceded, the usual furrows of skepticism on his brow softening. "Maybe our killer wanted an audience. Or imagined he had one."

"Then Hannah Grimes..." Carly's voice trailed off as she scanned the empty seats, visualizing the unseen observers to a macabre show. "She could be the third victim in a chain of performative acts."

"I still think it's possible it's unrelated," Gray decided, breaking the eerie silence. "But there's enough here now that I think we should pursue it as part of a string of cases. The difference in stab count could be because this one was a copycat."

Carly's eyes narrowed as she scrutinized the photos in her hands, each depicting a different crime scene yet unified by an unsettling similarity. Emily. Sarah. Hannah. The brisk wind whispered through the trees, carrying with it the chill of the unsolved and the scent of decay from the dilapidated amphitheater. Her breath clouded before her, dissipating quickly as if fearful of lingering too long at the scene.

"Emily was found here," Carly said, pointing to the first photo where the young woman lay against the natural backdrop, Lake Michigan stretching beyond the treeline like a slumbering giant. "And Sarah... there," she continued, gesturing towards a second image showcasing a valley yawning expansively behind the outline of another life stolen.

"Both positioned deliberately, almost artistically," Gray noted, his voice steady but tinged with the gravity of their gruesome context.

"Exactly," Carly affirmed. "And now, Hannah Grimes." She held up a third photograph, her thumb partially obscuring the corner as if trying to hold back the bleak truth within. "Her body was discovered right here, between the treeline we just came from and this amphitheater"

She stepped closer to Gray, her gaze reflecting the stark reality they faced. The amphitheater, once vibrant, now loomed silent and watchful among the trees, its forgotten purpose a haunting echo in their investigation.

"Notice anything?" Carly prodded, her gaze never wavering from Gray's.

He considered the images, seemingly analyzing them with a practiced eye that had seen too much yet missed very little. "The tree lines are constants, the vastness opposing them variable—a lake, a valley, now... an abandoned stage."

"Right," Carly said, a grim satisfaction in her voice. "It's like he's staging these murders, recreating something from his mind. A painting or a scene that only he understands fully—a body juxtaposed with nature's grandeur on one side and emptiness on the other."

"Or perhaps not emptiness," Gray mused, his mind working through the implications. "But rather, something that used to be full of life, full of observers."

"An unseen audience for a spectacle of one," Carly concluded, her lips pressing into a thin line. The thought sent a shiver down her spine that had nothing to do with the cold. She could almost hear the phantom applause, feel the anticipation of a crowd that would never witness the horrors laid bare before them.

The connection tethered them to a killer whose tool was cruelty, whose technique was violence. As they stood amid the silence of the amphitheater, Carly felt the weight of unspoken stories pressing upon her, the urgency to give voice to those who no longer could.

Gray's voice cut through the winter chill, decisive. "We should try to contact some of the people who gave statements in the case records." Carly nodded, her mind already sifting through potential leads as they headed back to her car, parked under the skeletal branches of leafless trees.

Once inside the vehicle, Gray flipped open the manila folder, and his finger traced down the list of names until it paused. "Here," he said, tapping on the paper. "Wendy Richardson, fellow nurse, friend of Hannah's. Lived at 18 Wind Oak Avenue."

"Let's see if she's still around." Carly's thumbs flew over the screen of her phone, a dancing ballet of digital inquiry. Moments later, she held a slip of information like a fragile hope. "Got a number."

"Give it a shot," Gray encouraged, his eyes steady on Carly, showing an inkling of trust that was hard-earned.

Carly drew in a deep breath before dialing, feeling the gravity of the years stretching between the present moment and the day Hannah Grimes' life had been cut short. The line clicked, and then, a voice, worn by time yet clear, answered.

"Hello?"

"Ms. Richardson?"

"Speaking. I don't accept cold calls, I'm sorry."

"No Ms. Richardson. This is Agent Carly Phoenix with the FBI. I'm looking into the murder of Hannah Grimes."

There was a pause on the other end, a hiccup of silence that carried the weight of memory. "Hannah was a lovely person," Wendy's voice finally emerged, tinged with old grief. "It broke all of us when we lost her... Her killer was never found. Tell me something has changed?"

Carly felt the echo of Wendy's loss resonate within her own chest, a hollow note that underscored the importance of their search. "I'm sorry for bringing this up after so long, but we're chasing a new lead."

"Anything to help," came the reply, weary yet willing.

"Can you think of anything unusual that happened in the run-up to Hannah's murder?" Carly asked, her voice soft but insistent, a coaxing thread trying to unravel the secrets of the past.

"Nothing comes to mind," Wendy responded slowly, each word measured against decades-old recollections. "Everything seemed normal until... until it wasn't."

Carly pressed the phone against her ear, the soft hum of static bridging the years between now and 1987. "Ms. Richardson, one more question if you don't mind. Was Hannah an artist herself?"

Wendy's voice crackled with the weight of memories. "No, Hannah didn't have an artistic bone in her body, bless her soul. But... oh, what was his name? She did mention seeing a local artist a few times."

"Can you remember anything about him?" Carly probed, her gaze flicking to Gray, who was watching her intently.

"I never met the man," Wendy admitted, a tinge of regret in her tone. "But I do recall them going out to this bar where the artsy crowd hung out. The Oval Portrait, it was called. Like the Poe story."

"Can you recall anything else? Anything at all?" Carly asked, more in hope than expectancy.

"No, I'm sorry. It was so long ago, you see," Wendy answered, mournfully. "It was so cruel, and just before she was about to be made a senior nurse at the hospital. She would have been terrific."

"Thank you, Ms. Richardson. You've been very helpful." Carly signaled the end of the call. "We'll be in touch if there's anything else we think you can assist us with."

"I hope you catch him," Wendy said. "He… He's been out there too long, knowing that he got away with it. Goodbye."

Gray's eyes were on Carly, expectant.

"What now?" he asked, the question simple but loaded with the gravity of their search.

"We need to find the bar Hannah used to frequent with her artist suitor," Carly stated without hesitation, determination etching her features.

She could feel the gears of the case shifting, a picture slowly coming into focus from the scattered fragments they had gathered. The Oval Portrait, a haven for artists and perhaps, a stage for a killer who painted in strokes of violence and left his grim works for the world to find.

CHAPTER TWELVE

Carly studied the neon glow that bathed the sidewalk, painting a sharp contrast to the creeping dusk. "The Oval Portrait" once hung above this spot in elegant cursive; now "Retro Recall" screamed in vibrant colors, its arcade charm beckoning the young and nostalgic. Carly turned to her partner, Gray, whose eyes were fixed on the blinking facade.

"Kind of looks more like an arcade than a bar, doesn't it?" she observed, attempting to pierce the professional veneer that Gray perpetually wore like armor. "But according to records, this is where The Oval Portrait used to be. It means Hannah was here."

He glanced at her briefly, the corners of his mouth twitching in what could be the beginning of a smile—or a grimace. "Arcades weren't really my scene," he replied, his voice steady as ever. "Dungeons and Dragons was more my speed."

She chuckled. "That figures." Her tone was light, but Carly's mind was anything but at ease. The past clung to this place like cobwebs, undisturbed for decades. Hannah Grimes had walked through these doors, unknowingly towards her doom, after her shift at the hospital.

"Let's see what we can find out about Hannah's last night here," Gray suggested, stepping toward the entrance. But even as they crossed the threshold, Carly knew that Retro Recall bore no resemblance to its former self, the rustic Oval Portrait now long since faded into history and replaced with a time capsule, a tribute to 1980s arcades.

Inside, Carly couldn't help but let her façade slip, revealing a flicker of excitement as she took in the interior. The air hummed with electronic beeps and synthesized music, a wave of nostalgia played out across rows of vintage arcade machines. Their screens flickered with pixelated promises from the 80s and 90s, drawing in patrons like moths to a flame.

"Look at all these cabinets," Carly said, her voice tinged with genuine admiration. She allowed herself a momentary escape, picturing the joy of losing herself in the simple challenge of high scores and digital conquests. "I'd be happy to stay here and play the lot if I wasn't on duty."

Gray gave her a sidelong glance, a hint of amusement breaking through. "Focus, Phoenix," he said, though the teasing note in his voice softened the reprimand. "We're not here for games."

"Right." Carly nodded, snapping back to the gravity of their mission. Behind the flashing lights and sounds of virtual battles, the specter of Hannah Grimes lingered. This was not a place of innocent amusement for Carly—it was potentially the hunting ground of a killer, the backdrop to a tragedy that refused to be confined to the past.

Carly's gaze followed Gray as he navigated through the maze of arcade machines, his figure a stark contrast to the patrons bathed in the glow of neon screens. His determined stride didn't falter, even as the playful energy of Retro Recall buzzed around him. He was a man on a mission, and Carly knew better than to get in his way.

Approaching the bar, Gray flagged down one of the bartenders, a young woman with hair dyed in a rainbow of colors that shimmered under the bar lights. "We need to speak to the manager," he stated, his voice carrying the weight of authority that demanded attention.

"Sure thing," she chirped, slipping past them to disappear through a door marked 'Staff Only.' Moments later, she returned with a man who looked more like a band front man than a bar manager. His jeans were ripped in all the fashionably right places, his t-shirt emblazoned with a logo for a band Carly had never heard of.

"Ralph Jinx," he introduced himself with a grin that revealed a silver canine tooth. "What can I do for you?"

"Jinx?" Gray raised an eyebrow. "Is that a nickname or?.."

"Real name," Ralph cut in, tapping a rhythm on the bar top. "Changed it for my band."

Carly couldn't help but laugh, a soft snort that she quickly smothered. "That figures," she muttered, sharing a knowing look with Gray. The world they had stepped into was a far cry from the sterile corridors of the FBI field office.

Gray drew a breath, the playful ambiance not swaying his focus. "We're investigating a murder from nearly forty years ago. A woman named Hannah Grimes used to come here when it was the Oval Portrait. She was seeing an artist not long before she died. They used to drink here together."

Carly watched Ralph closely, searching for any flicker of recognition.

"Wow, that's... way before my time," Ralph said with a shrug, unfazed. "But an artist that kills, huh? Sounds like it could be a cool idea for a song."

"Her death isn't material for your next hit, Mr. Jinx," Carly interjected sharply, her expression hardening. "It's as real today as it was back then. It's someone's life we're talking about."

The carefree smirk faded from Ralph's face, replaced with a sudden sobriety. "Yeah, I get that. Sorry, I—"

"Apology accepted," Carly cut him off, and turned to Gray. "Let's not waste any more time here."

They moved away from the bar, leaving Ralph to ponder the gravity of their visit. As they threaded back through the digital cacophony, Carly's mind raced. The artist, the connection to Hannah, it was a clue hanging just out of reach, taunting her. She needed to dive deeper, immerse herself in the victim's world if she was going to catch a killer who seemed as spectral as the electronic ghosts blinking on the arcade screens.

Gray's gaze lingered on the neon-lit sign of Retro Recall on the wall, a mocking hint of nostalgia in his eyes. "We're running in circles here," he finally said, turning to Carly. "There's nothing left here to unearth. Let's head back and dive into the files again."

Carly leaned against the cool metal wall of the bar, her mind churning with images of Hannah Grimes, her fate woven into the fabric of this transformed place. "When I was with the BAU," she began, her voice steady but distant, "I learned an immersion technique from Jack Fritz—before he went off the reservation. Helped me get inside the headspace of victims... sometimes even the killers."

"Jack's methods are controversial," Gray acknowledged, clearly having heard of them, shifting from one foot to another, uneasy at the prospect of unconventional tactics. "But if you think it could give us an edge..."

"Sometimes you have to step outside the lines to see the full picture," Carly replied.

Gray grumbled something under his breath about procedure and the reliability of good old-fashioned legwork, but Carly saw the subtle nod, giving her silent permission to proceed as she saw fit.

"Why don't you go back to the office?" she said, pushing off the wall to face him squarely. "I'm going to stay for a while, try to connect with Hannah's last moments here. Get into her head space."

"Using the Fritz Method as an excuse to hit the arcade cabinets?" Gray's tone was playful but laced with skepticism.

"Only if Ms. Pac-Man can offer up some clues," Carly shot back with a half-smile, watching Gray shake his head as he walked away, his figure soon swallowed by the growing shadows of the evening.

Alone now, Carly let the sounds of the arcade wash over her—the electronic beeps and bloops, the triumphant cheers over high scores achieved, the low murmur of conversations imbued with laughter and drink. But beneath it all was a silent undercurrent, a connection to a terrible crime, perhaps three or more.

She claimed a stool at the bar, the surface worn smooth by countless hands before hers—a touchstone to the history of the place. Her eyes scanned the room, soaking in the details. Each joystick and button, each flickering screen held untold stories, echoes of joy and escape. Somewhere in this mix of pixels and nostalgia lay the answers to a riddle decades old.

Carly knew the immersion had begun, her mind reaching back across the years, searching for the shadows cast by a killer who had walked among these very machines, who had courted death as deftly as the gamers courted victory. She needed to find him, to understand his motives and movements, to anticipate his next move before another life was lost to his twisted game. And so she sat, the huntress cloaked in the guise of revelry, her eyes alight with the fire of determination. The game was on.

Carly perched on the worn leather of the bar stool, her posture rigid with purpose. She inhaled deeply, the scent of aged wood and electronic ozone filling her senses, grounding her in the now before she dove into the then. Her fingers traced the edge of her glass, condensation beading beneath her touch as her mind began to drift.

Eyes closed, she cast herself back, embodying Hannah Grimes with an empath's precision. She felt the weight of a nurse's responsibility, the lives saved and lost, the balance of joy and sorrow that left one feeling hollowed out at the end of a shift. She imagined the comfort found in a man whose world was painted in broad strokes of color and passion, so different from the sterile whites and grays of her own.

Yet, as Carly conjured the scene of their last meeting, there was no warmth in the imagined embrace. She saw Hannah walking toward the amphitheater, anticipation humming through her. The trust in her steps, her belief in connection, all shattered by the stark revelation of a blade glinting in the twilight. In her mind's eye, Carly flinched as the final truth cut deeper than any knife could—Hannah's love had been a weapon wielded against her, the artist's affection nothing but a shadow puppet's dance orchestrated by death itself.

The clinking of glasses snapped Carly back, and she opened her eyes to the neon-infused reality of Retro Recall. The juxtaposition was jarring—a colorful facade masking the complexity of human nature. She let the ambiance of the arcade wash over her, the playful sounds a stark counterpoint to the somber task at hand.

Still seated at the bar, Carly shifted her mental gears, now allowing the visage of the artist to take shape within her thoughts. A creator turned destroyer, his failures a gnawing emptiness that consumed him. What drove a man, whose vocation was to bring beauty into the world, to snuff out the light of promising futures?

She pondered Emily, the young talent with a vibrant spark extinguished too soon. Sarah, the successful executive who had climbed the ranks with tenacity and vision. And Hannah, who had dedicated her life to nurturing others, only to have it ripped away cruelly, just before a looming promotion.

Each woman's story was a reminder of what the artist could never attain. Their successes were silent rebukes to his inadequacies, their achievements the milestones he'd never reach. Carly's gaze hardened as the pieces fell into place, the mosaic of motive taking form before her. These women weren't just victims; they were mirrors reflecting back the killer's own shortcomings—a truth he sought to shatter with each life taken.

Carly's fingers tapped an impatient rhythm against the bar's worn surface, her mind churning with the revelations that surged through her like a current. The cacophony of electronic beeps and synthesized music from the arcade cabinets provided an incongruous backdrop to the grim puzzle pieces assembling in her head. The neon lights cast vibrant hues across her face as she pieced together the dark mosaic of a killer's motive.

Ambition. Success. These were the attributes that had marked Emily, Sarah, and Hannah for death. It was envy, pure and corrosive, that compelled their murderer—an artist who could not bear the reflection of his own mediocrity in the glow of their accomplishments. His method was one of carnage, each stroke a violent retort to a world that had acknowledged them but overlooked him.

With a surge of adrenaline, Carly stood abruptly, her chair scraping back with a jarring screech that cut through the digital embrace of the arcade. She had no time for games—not when lives were at stake, and certainly not when she was this close to understanding the twisted psyche driving their suspect.

The agent wove through clusters of patrons, her stride purposeful and swift as she passed by aisles of flashing screens and animated chatter. Outside, the evening had begun to settle over Chicago, wrapping the city in its dusky shroud, but Carly's mind was alight, ablaze with the urgency of her epiphany.

She burst through the door of Retro Recall, the cool air grazing her skin as the sounds of the arcade faded behind her. The streets were alive with the thrum of rush hour traffic and the discordant melodies of urban life, but Carly was attuned only to the singular focus of her mission.

As she hailed a cab with the practiced ease of an agent always on the move, Carly's thoughts raced ahead to Gray. He needed to hear her theory, to understand that they weren't just chasing a random killer from the past—they were hunting a man fueled by resentment and failure. A man who had turned his impotence into a weapon against those who dared to shine brighter than he ever could.

Carly knew they may not have the name of a suspect just yet, but they at least had a motive.

CHAPTER THIRTEEN

Carly stepped into Espresso Dreams, a cafe that seemed to resist the march of time with its aged bronze fixtures and mahogany counters, all steeped in the aroma of dark roasted beans. The walls adorned with local art for sale were bathed in the subdued light seeping through the stained-glass windows, giving off an amber hue that lent the space an air of comfort against the Chicago chill.

"Gray," she called out, spotting her partner tucked away in a corner booth, his briefcase a stoic companion by his feet.

Michael Grayson looked up, his eyes briefly scanning the bustling space before settling on Carly with a quizzical expression. "Interesting place… Why here?" he asked as she slid into the seat across from him.

"Thought it might help to get out of the office for a bit," Carly replied, glancing at the menu despite already knowing what she wanted.

Gray nodded slowly, signaling the waiter before turning his attention back to Carly. "I'll have a cappuccino," he said, then eyed her choice as she ordered an espresso. "Trying to quit coffee and smoking simultaneously is probably a bad idea."

"Quitting both?" Carly leaned forward, resting her elbows on the table. Her stare fixed on him with a mixture of concern and curiosity. "Why the sudden change?"

"I'm 43," Gray sighed, rubbing the stubble shadowing his jaw.

"That's still young?" Carly asked, puzzled.

"As one cinematic hero once put it, it's not the years, but the mileage. My senses, they're not what they used to be. I need every edge I can get to keep my mind sharp." His voice carried an undercurrent of discipline that Carly couldn't help but respect. Carly often realized that she was a fiery personality who led with her gut, and while that worked most of the time, she hoped one day to be less impulsive.

It was impulsiveness that landed her a demotion to the Chicago field office.

"Commitment like that's admirable," she said genuinely. Then, with a tilt of her head, she ventured further. "I don't know much about you,

Gray. Are you married? Have family?"

"Married? No," Gray exhaled softly, the steam from the arriving cappuccino curling around his words. "But I do have a son, Maxwell."

"I don't know if I'm cut out for family bliss. Must be nice, though, having a kid," Carly mused, cradling her espresso cup in her hands.

"Sometimes," Gray said wistfully, a smile flickering and fading fast. "It is a privilege to watch them grow, but an open wound when they won't talk to you."

"Trouble communicating?" she probed gently.

"Maxwell's birth was... tough. Katrina, his mother, died in childbirth. I did my best to raise the boy while climbing the ladder at the FBI." Gray sipped his cappuccino, wincing slightly at the heat. "I didn't always make the best calls."

Carly watched Gray's eyes cloud over with a mix of regret and resolve. It was strange to see the chinks in his armor, the glimpses of the man behind the badge. She knew the cost of their line of work, the sacrifices made, and the personal lives often left in disarray. They were more alike than she had first believed, each marked by loss and a relentless pursuit of answers that sometimes led them down paths no one else would tread.

"Raising a kid on your own can't be easy," she said softly, letting the conversation breathe, realizing that beneath the procedural veneer, Gray was as human as they came, worn by time and duty, yet still standing.

Carly observed the way Gray's gaze drifted to the streaks of rain on the cafe window, his mind clearly elsewhere. She took a slow sip of her espresso, the bitter liquid grounding her thoughts.

"What about you, Phoenix? Any family?" he finally asked as if awakening from a spell.

For a moment, she almost lied. But she felt strangely open for the first time. "A brother," she said before he could ask any more. "His name is Justin. I was left to look after him. It was just us after our mother passed. I was barely an adult myself. Still a kid in many ways, though not in the eyes of the law."

"Sorry to hear that," he murmured.

"Life dealt its hand," Carly replied with a shrug. "I had to grow up fast, look after him. It wasn't always smooth sailing." A shadow of her former life fluttered across her memory—the struggles, the responsibilities that matured her too quickly.

"Sounds like you understand a bit of what it's like... making sacrifices for family," Gray stated, connecting the dots between their lives. "You grew up around here, didn't you?"

Cary was surprised that he could tell, as she had never mentioned it. In fact, it was something she hid. Not because she was ashamed of the city, but rather that to pretend she came from elsewhere, allowed her to bury the pain of the past.

"Chicago, born and bred," she confirmed, watching as surprise registered on his face. The city had shaped her, honed her skills like the biting winter winds sculpted the skyline.

"That could be useful," Gray admitted, a hint of respect lacing his words. "Local connections might give us an edge on our cases. I've been here for several years, but you never quite get a sense for a place entirely unless you spend your formative years there."

"Speaking of the case," Gray segued with the ease of someone who'd spent years weaving through conversations like a boxer dodging punches. "Did Fritz's immersion technique at the Retro Recall bar help at all?"

"More than I expected," Carly acknowledged, feeling the pieces of the puzzle aligning in her mind. "I think I've started to crack the victim profile. Went deeper into Emily's background—we know through Fleming at Art déco that she was displaying her art at fundraisers, right in the heart of local projects."

"Indeed," Gray mused, leaning forward, seemingly captivated by the thread she was unraveling

"Then there's Sarah Jennings," Carly continued, the cogs turning. "She was neck-deep in the business community. And Hannah Grimes..." She paused, remembering Wendy's offhand comment that now blazed like a neon sign. "She was on the cusp of becoming a Senior Nurse before she died."

"Patterns," Gray muttered, his detective's mind clearly ticking over each fact.

"Think about it," Carly pressed on, her tone firm but hushed, as if the walls might be listening. "Ambitious women, successful, rising stars in their fields... and then they're snuffed out. What if the killer targeted them because of his own inadequacies? Striking at what he can't have or be."

Gray absorbed her theory, his expression unreadable for a moment. She knew she was onto something—she could feel the electric charge of a breakthrough. The killer wasn't just ending lives; he was quenching the light of potential, extinguishing flames that burned brighter than his own. It was personal, a twisted form of leveling the playing field where he felt most inadequate.

Gray nodded, his eyes a shade darker as the weight of Carly's analysis settled over them. "You've got something here," he agreed, his voice steady but with an edge that mirrored the tension in the cramped confines of Espresso Dreams. "Perhaps there is more to Fritz's immersion techniques than I thought."

The aroma of freshly ground coffee beans was pervasive, wrapping around them like an invisible shroud as they dissected the killer's pattern. Cups chinked nearby as a dozen conversations whispered around them from other booths.

"Thirteen times," Gray said suddenly, his gaze drifting past Carly to the rain-smeared window. A chill seemed to pass through her as she followed his line of sight to the gray Chicago sky. "Emily and Sarah, both stabbed thirteen times. That fact can't be a coincidence. As well as your ambition profile, maybe there's a superstition at play, or some compulsion driving him. It suggests a meticulousness, doesn't it? An obsessive nature."

Carly considered this, her espresso forgotten and cooling rapidly on the scarred wooden table between them. "Obsessive Compulsive Disorder could explain the precision," she mused, tapping her finger against her lips. "And if he is superstitious, that might be another angle we can use to understand him, predict his moves. It could explain why he's trying to create something with each kill, laying the bodies in similar places, letting them freeze in the cold."

Gray leaned back, the old wood creaking under his weight. His eyes were distant, thoughtful, and Carly knew that familiar look—the sign of gears churning in the methodical mind of a seasoned investigator. Then, reaching into his briefcase, he pulled out a worn manila folder, the edges frayed from age and handling.

"Your breakthrough isn't the only one we've had," Gray announced, flipping the folder open to reveal a sheet of faded paper. He slid it across the table. "I was going through more of Hannah's files. A note from a previous investigator during the 80s caught my eye."

Carly leaned forward, scanning the note. It spoke of Hannah's sudden interest in art, a detail that pricked at Carly's heightened intuitions.

"An art class?" she echoed, her voice sharp with curiosity. "At Eagle College?"

"According to her mother." Gray's deep voice carried a gravity that underscored the potential significance of the lead. "Hannah been attending for weeks before her death."

The implications raced through Carly's mind like the wailing of passing squad cars. Art... again. First Emily, an artist, then Sarah, an art enthusiast and fundraiser, and finally Hannah, newly drawn to the artistic world of color and contrast. The pattern was there, stark and undeniable. It was like the killer was painting his own macabre portrait with the blood of his victims, each one a stroke of his twisted masterpiece.

Carly knew the conclusion: Was art the means through which he met his victims?

"An art class could mean he's someone who blends in, someone who's part of that scene," Carly said, her thoughts crystallizing into a plan of action. "We have to look into this, Gray. Whoever was teaching that class, the students... they could give us a name, a face, if they are still around."

Gray nodded, the document in his hands seeming to pulse with potential. "And if our killer felt overshadowed by these women, art might be where he's trying to prove himself. Where he feels powerful enough to take lives. That could be why he laid the bodies out, trying to make art of his own, which supersedes the endeavors of his victims. This class could be pivotal."

"Then hopefully that's where we'll find him," Carly declared, determination steeling her voice. She felt it in her bones; they were close to something new, so close to pulling this shadowy figure into the light. And when they did, all his careful patterns and compulsions would be his undoing.

"Hold on a second," she said, pulling out her phone.

Carly's fingers danced over the screen of her phone, the motion fluid and practiced. The art department at Eagle College emerged in a search result, an anchor point in a sea of digital noise. She looked up at Gray, alight with the spark of revelation. "The art department is still there. I wonder…"

"Most colleges are duty bound to keep records of their students, to verify their accomplishments later," Gray echoed thoughtfully, his gaze sharpening.

"Exactly," Carly insisted, her voice carrying the vibrancy of her deduction. Now her thoughts were racing, eking out a pathway to a solution. Sometimes it was like being possessed by a thought, like a question that had to be answered. Another assertion quickly found space in her mind. "Due you remember the phone call with Hannah's friend? Wendy mentioned Hannah dating an artist before she died. It fits too well to be a coincidence."

"It's possible that very artist is either the killer or someone who, unknowingly or not, facilitated the killer's introduction to the victims," Gray conceded, his skepticism momentarily suspended by the plausibility of Carly's theory.

"Look here—" Carly tilted the screen of her phone toward Gray. "A man named Arthur Welling heads the department. We should talk to him, see if he has any records from back then."

"Old files can be like finding needles in haystacks," Gray mused aloud, but Carly detected no defeat in his tone.

"Then let's bring a magnet," she quipped, pocketing her phone as she rose from the table, her coffee cup empty save for the mocha-colored stain at its bottom.

Gray nodded, casting a last glance at the cozy clutter of Espresso Dreams. Carly felt it, too. The cafe had been a brief respite from the chaos of their investigation, but now it felt confining, too quaint for the unseen threat they were chasing.

"Let's roll," Carly urged, her stride purposeful as they exited into the chill Chicago air. A gust tugged at her hair, whipping strands across her face. She brushed them away, her mind already on the steps ahead.

Eagle College awaited, and in its archives, Carly hoped to find the name of the killer.

CHAPTER FOURTEEN

Carly squinted against the stark brightness of the frozen afternoon sun as she and Gray approached the sprawling campus of Eagle College. The institution wore its prestige like an aged patina, its red-brick buildings crowned with weathered copper spires that seemed to pierce the sky. Between them, manicured lawns sprawled out like green oceans, peppered with students who drifted in clusters, their laughter riding the breeze.

"This place probably hasn't changed much since Hannah was here," Carly mused aloud, her gaze taking in the antiquated sights and architecture.

Gray simply grunted in response, his attention fixed on the doorway ahead.

Entering the administration building, a hush swallowed their footsteps. The receptionist, a woman with a stern bun and glasses perched on her nose, lifted her gaze from behind a computer screen. Carly flashed her badge smoothly, the motion practiced and precise.

"Agents Phoenix and Grayson, FBI," she announced, the words causing a subtle tightening around the receptionist's eyes. "We need to speak with Arthur Welling, head of the art department."

"Is he expecting you?" The receptionist's voice held an edge of caution, her fingers hovering over the keyboard as if ready to summon an invisible barrier.

"No, but it's urgent," Carly replied, her tone leaving no room for debate.

The receptionist hesitated, then sighed, picking up the phone with reluctant fingers. After a brief exchange, she hung up and gestured towards a hallway. "He's not in his office right now, but you can wait there. Second door to your left."

"Thank you," Gray said, his politeness incongruous with the grim set of his jaw.

They found Welling's office easily enough, the heavy wooden door ajar. Inside, the walls were a testament to the human form, adorned with framed nude paintings in various poses and styles. Carly let out a low whistle, her expression dancing with amusement.

"Looks like Welling has quite the... appreciation for the arts," she quipped, her gaze lingering on an oil painting of a reclining figure bathed in warm light.

"Are that many nude bodies really necessary?" Gray remarked.

"Oh, don't tell me you're a prude, Gray?" Carly said, laughing.

"There's a fine line between art and titillation. Some of these pieces are the latter."

Gray's cheeks colored ever so slightly, his discomfort palpable. "Let's just find what we came for and get out," he muttered, avoiding the walls as if they might come to life and scandalize him further.

Before Carly could tease her partner further, the door creaked open wider and Arthur Welling stepped in. He was a vision of academia gone to seed—thin, white hair wisped around a speckled scalp, his pale skin hanging loosely on a frame that once might have been robust. His clothes, though clean, were an ensemble of outdated tweeds and elbow patches, as if he had walked straight out of a different era.

"Agents?" Welling's voice was thin but carried an undercurrent of authority. "I'm Arthur Welling. How can I assist the FBI today?"

His eyes, sharp beneath bushy gray brows, flickered between Carly and Gray, assessing them with the critical eye of a man accustomed to scrutinizing finer details. But Carly noted something else—a tightness around his mouth, the faintest frown lines indicating that this unexpected visit was more than a mere inconvenience. She sensed a story buried deep within those weary lines, one that could lead to the darker truths they were seeking.

"We're investigating a multiple homicide," Gray said.

Arthur Welling's congenial smile twitched at the corners as he leaned against the edge of his heavy oak desk, the varnish shining from years of attentive care. His gaze shifted from Carly to Gray, and a shadow seemed to pass across his face like a cloud veiling the sun. "Murder?" he echoed, the word hanging awkwardly in the air.

"Three women killed in the 1980s," Carly clarified, her voice steady, though she felt the undercurrent of urgency that always came with such cases. "A student who attended an art class here at Eagle College, Hannah Grimes, is one of the victims."

She watched Welling closely, her understanding of body language allowing her to pick apart the minute changes in his posture, the subtle tightening of his hands where they rested on the desk. The hint of defensiveness was almost imperceptible, but to Carly's discerning eye, it was as glaring as a neon sign. Her gut prickled; there was something beneath his academic veneer that didn't want to be unearthed.

Gray cleared his throat, bringing the room back into focus. "We have reason to believe Hannah attended a night class here at the art department, somewhere between late '86 and early '87." He pulled out a notepad, flipping it open to a page marked with a small post-it. "We were hoping you might assist us by providing the class roll for those sessions."

Welling's eyes narrowed slightly, his lips pressed into a thin line. "I'm sure you understand, Agent Grayson, that our students' privacy is paramount. I can't just hand over confidential information without proper authorization."

"Of course," Gray replied, sternness etched into his words. "But you see—"

"However," Carly interjected, sensing the rehearsed nature of Welling's refusal, "the situation is quite serious. We're looking into a series of murders, and any help you could provide would be invaluable to our investigation. It's possible the killer was a fellow student of Hannah's. In fact, it may be likely. We won't know until we look at the class roll."

Her gaze didn't waver, locking onto Welling's with an intensity that commanded cooperation. She saw the flicker of something in his expression, a brief glimpse of what might have been fear or perhaps guilt. Carly knew that look well—it was the look of a man who had something to hide.

Arthur Welling looked increasingly uncomfortable. "I'm afraid I still…"

"Then we'll secure a warrant and have the college shut down for a few days while we go through your archives," Carly stated, her voice edged with iron determination. She studied Arthur Welling's face as she spoke, noting the beads of sweat that had begun to collect along his hairline despite the controlled coolness of the office air. A man used to curating beauty now stood marred by the ugliness of stress.

"Please… That won't be necessary," he said, looking almost ill at the suggestion.

"Do you know of the night class Hannah attended?" she asked, watching him closely.

Welling hesitated, his eyes flicking away for an instant before returning to meet hers. "The records from that period... they wouldn't be digitized," he muttered, more to himself than to the agents. "I'll have to look for the physical file in our archives. They are just down the hall. Give me a few minutes, please."

Once he excused himself, leaving behind a silence heavy with unspoken suspicions, Carly turned to Gray with a skeptical arch of her brow.

"Something's off," Carly said the moment the door clicked shut behind Welling. The office seemed to close in around them, every painting on the wall bearing silent witness to their confrontation.

"Arthur's hiding something, Gray. He's like a cornered fox—ready to bolt."

Gray shifted uncomfortably, his gaze lingering where Welling had stood. "I'm not sure," he responded, his voice carrying the weight of his procedural caution. "Could be nothing. Running an art department can't be easy. There's a lot of pressure, and you just poured fuel onto it with your threats. I don't approve of that."

"Trust me," Carly insisted, her face sharp with the intuition honed from years at the BAU. "I've seen this dance before—suspects getting jittery before they make a run for it. I'm going to follow him."

"Alright," Gray conceded, though his doubt lingered like a shadow. "I'll stay here, keep an eye out in case he actually comes back."

But Carly was already moving towards the door, her steps silent and purposeful. She knew better than to wait for a suspect to return—if Welling was going to make a move, it would be now, while he thought they were still waiting in his office, wrapped up in the false sense of security he tried to weave with his reluctance and excuses. She could feel the adrenaline beginning to surge, the hunter instinct within her awakening.

Carly's steps were silent, her mind a focused blade as she tracked Arthur Welling through the dimly lit halls of Eagle College. The aging corridors seemed to echo with secrets, the musty scent of old paper and forgotten history hanging heavy in the air. She moved with the fluid grace of a predator, her intuitions taking over as she slipped from shadow to shadow.

The archives room loomed ahead, a cavern of records and relics. Carly watched as Welling slipped inside, his movements furtive, his shoulders hunched beneath the weight of his deeds. She allowed herself a moment, listening for the sound of the shredder—a mechanical growl amidst the silence.

She edged into the doorway, her eyes narrowing as she saw him, hands trembling as they started to feed the class roll into the shredder's hungry maw. The pieces of Hannah Grimes' past—her connections, her presence—were being torn away, reduced to confetti by a man desperate to erase his own.

“Stop!” she commanded, her voice cutting through the noise. But Welling had already seen her reflection in the dusty glass of a framed diploma, his eyes widening in the realization that he had been caught.

Arthur bolted, his surprisingly agile form disappearing through an adjacent door, leaving behind the choked whir of the shredder as Carly whisked the mostly intact evidence out of it. Then she turned and gave chase, her heart thundering in rhythm with her footsteps as she rushed through hallways and corridors of the college.

Welling was faster than his age would have suggested, his desperation lending wings to his feet, but Carly was relentless. Her every stride was efficient, honed from years of pursuit, her mind calculating routes and angles even as she ran. The gap between them ebbed and flowed as they darted through the long hallways and the shadows cast by the intermittent windows.

Then, out of nowhere, something small and gleaming tore through the stillness of the corridor, striking Arthur on the side of the head with a precision that was almost athletic in of itself. His balance faltered, his arms windmilling as he stumbled and went down hard on the unforgiving floor tiles.

Carly was upon him in an instant, her handcuffs clicking shut with the finality of a vault door sealing.

“You’re being detained,” she said, breathing heavily.

Welling lay there, the fight draining from him as quickly as it had surged, his breaths coming in ragged gasps. Carly stood, her chest heaving, a thin sheen of sweat on her brow, her gaze fixed on the figure who had thrown the decisive blow.

Gray’s small grin was the punctuation mark at the end of a breathless sentence. He leaned against the frame of the doorway, his eyebrows raised in a silent ‘gotcha’ as Carly snapped cuffs on Arthur Welling’s wrists. She straightened up and noticed the silver object that had turned the chase—a weighty metal pen lying innocently on the floor.

“Good aim,” Carly said, her tone light despite the adrenaline still flowing through her.

“Always preferred penmanship to running,” Gray quipped, bending down to retrieve the projectile.

“Looks like this pen could double as a weapon.” Carly joked, turning the hefty object over in her hand.

“Ah, but don’t forget,” Gray said, helping her haul Welling to his feet, “the pen is mightier than the sword.”

“You are most definitely a dad with jokes like that,” she said.

"Come on, help me with Arthur here. We're going to have a nice chat."

Back in the art department head's office, Carly propped Welling into a chair. His pale skin had taken on a sheen of sweat, his thin white hair plastered to his forehead. The room felt smaller with tension, every nude painting on the wall an audience to the unfolding drama.

"Arthur," Carly began, "Why were you shredding the class roll?"

Welling's gaze flickered away for a moment before meeting hers again. "I don't want to go to jail," he murmured, as if the words themselves were capable of shackling him.

"Whether you do or not isn't up to me," Carly replied coolly. "But it will depend on what you tell us." Her stare fixed on his, unwavering.

"I think you or someone you know were on that class roll, Arthur. Am I right?" Her voice was steady, but the question hung in the air with the gravity of a verdict waiting to be delivered.

Welling's Adam's apple bobbed as he swallowed hard, the lines of age etched into his face seemed to deepen. "Yes," he admitted finally. "I was."

Carly nodded, her mind already racing ahead. This was another piece of the puzzle, one that brought them closer to the killer's identity, one that tightened the net around a past that someone wanted desperately to keep buried.

Gray's voice cut through the charged air, bringing Arthur Welling back from the brink of his inner turmoil. "Were you the instructor for that class, Arthur? Or a student?"

Welling's hands trembled slightly as he clasped them together, an attempt to still his nerves or perhaps to conjure a protective barrier between himself and the truth. "I—I was a student," he stammered out, the confession falling flat in the heavy silence that enveloped the office.

Carly leaned forward, her hair catching the light filtering in from the window, giving her an almost ethereal glow against the stark backdrop of Welling's cluttered office.

"Did you start seeing Hannah before her death?" she asked, her tone gentle yet unyielding, coaxing the repressed fears to surface. "We know she was seeing an artist."

"Yes," Welling whispered, as if the admission itself pained him. "But I didn't kill her. I panicked when I realized they you might connect us…I just wanted to get rid of anything that could lead back to me."

"Arthur," Carly said, her gaze not wavering from his face, reading every tic, every shift of his pale eyes. "Did you frequent The Oval Portrait bar around the time Hannah died? Were you drinking with here there that night?"

"No!"

"But you did frequent there?" Gray pushed.

He nodded, a resigned slump falling over his shoulders—a puppet whose strings had been cut. "Sometimes, but it wasn't like it seems. I asked around after Hannah died. One of the bartenders there told me he saw her with another man the night she…passed. I swear it wasn't me."

"Did you ever tell the police that?" Carly probed further, her mind already sifting through the implications of this new information.

Welling shook his head, the motion slow, burdened by the weight of his choices. "No. I knew how it would look. I was already involved with her, so naturally, they would consider me a suspect. And… I had a wife at the time. I didn't want her finding out. Hannah didn't know about her."

That comment sparked a thought in Carly's mind. "That gives you motive to kill her, if she did know. Was she going to ruin your marriage, Arthur?"

"No! I swear she didn't know," he said. "I'm an artist. I create. I don't destroy."

"Not even in the name of art?" Gray asked. "Perhaps you were making a grisly art project of your own with each kill."

"Please," he said, his voice trembling. "None of that is true."

"There's a simple way to put that to the test. Did you have an alibi for the night Hannah died, Arthur?" Carly pressed on, her voice steadfast, demanding honesty in a room filled with deceit.

His answer was a frail whisper, one that barely disturbed the air. "No. I was alone at my apartment that night while my wife was out of town. Another reason not to tell the police about my involvement with Hannah back then. I knew it wouldn't look good."

Carly sat back, processing the reluctant confessions that spilled from Welling's lips. Each word was a piece, some jagged, some smooth, and all fitting together to form a picture that was far from complete. Alone in his apartment—a statement, a truth, a lie. It was their job to discern which.

Gray's question sliced through the tension in the room like a scalpel, precise and probing. "Arthur, where were you on the 18th of November 1985 and the 21st of February 1986? Those are the dates when two other women, Emily Rosario and Sarah Jennings, were killed."

Welling's chest rose with a deep inhalation, his exhale carrying the weight of a man unburdening himself of suspicion. "I was in England then," he said, voice finding an unexpected steadiness. "Studying art. I didn't return to the states until December of '86 with my wife. She was from there." His thin hands moved almost reflexively to straighten the cuffs of his shirt, a gesture of a man clinging to the edges of composure.

"Can you prove that?" Carly asked, her gaze never wavering from his face, searching for the micro expressions that might betray a lie.

"Of course," Welling asserted, his pale eyes meeting hers with newfound vigor. "I have documents—passports, enrollment papers, sketches I made while abroad. They're all dated."

"Even if that's true," Carly countered, her tone even but firm, "it doesn't clear you for Hannah's murder."

"You could have been copying the previous two murders," Gray added.

"No," Welling replied. "I didn't kill Hannah or anyone else. For Christ's sake, I won't even kill an animal. I'm a vegetarian!"

"So was Hitler," Carly remarked. "You're going to have to come with us, Arthur. We'll get to the bottom of this, one way or another."

Carly's hand closed around Welling's wrist with practiced ease as she clamped the cold steel of the handcuffs around his bony appendage. She and Gray escorted him from the office, the air thick with unspoken questions and the musky scent of old books and fear.

Arthur said nothing, except a brief murmur of "I'll call my lawyer when we get there."

As they approached Gray's car, Carly's mind churned, dissecting Welling's every word, every inflection. With Welling secured in the backseat, she leaned against the cool metal of the vehicle, allowing herself a moment to glance at the sky, its vastness unerring compared to the narrow confines of their investigation.

"Gray," she said, turning to meet his steady gaze, "I don't think he's our guy. Welling mentioned another man—someone with Hannah the night she died. What if we've been looking at this all wrong?"

"Meaning?"

"Maybe it's not about the art classes, or the bars," Carly elaborated, her voice infused with a sudden intensity. "The other victims... Emily, Sarah... we should be examining their romantic encounters. Perhaps the killer targeted them because of the type of man they were dating. If there's a pattern, if someone was targeting them because of who they were seeing—"

"It could give us a whole new angle," Gray finished, nodding slowly, his mind already sifting through the implications.

Gray looked up at the sky. “Looks like snow is coming.”

“Let’s get Welling processed,” Carly suggested. “Even if he has an alibi, he still resisted arrest. Then someone else can deal with him and his lawyer.”

"I think it might be a good time to call it a day after that," Gray added. "Refresh our energies for the next day."

“I don’t want to stop,” Carly said, frustrated.

“You’re going to have to learn, Phoenix,” Gray said, calmly. “This isn’t an active fugitive case like your previous work at the BAU. These are cold cases. They can wait one more day.”

“Unless the killer is still active,” Carly said, getting into the car.

And that was a thought that didn’t bear thinking.

“Just a couple more hours?” Carly asked.

Gray nodded. “Then sleep.”

CHAPTER FIFTEEN

1988, Chicago. The year of the big freeze.

January's chill clung to the air like a persistent whisper of winter, biting and unwelcome. The park, blanketed in frost, was nearly empty save for the small knot of artists huddled over their canvasses, painting with enthusiasm that defied the cold. He watched them from his solitary bench, a silent observer shrouded in the anonymity of his heavy coat and scarf.

The killer's gaze drifted across the scene, his mind churning with dark thoughts that clashed starkly with the serene setting. The crisp air nipped at his exposed skin, a sensation he welcomed—an invigorating reminder of life, fleeting and precious. It was this time of year when his work thrived, when the concept of "The Perfect Frozen Abyss" consumed him.

Details of the abyss were enigmatic, even to him, but its allure was persistent. Each victim brought him closer to understanding, to perfection. His eyes narrowed as the vision of it danced behind his eyelids, an intimate secret between him and the call of death. He craved it—the artistry of the kill, the preservation of that final, frozen moment.

The surrounding park was quiet, save for the soft touches of brushes against paintings. He remained motionless, a phantom among the living, contemplating his next step towards the chilling masterpiece that awaited him—a masterpiece only complete with the cessation of a heartbeat.

He reveled in the way the cold sharpened his senses, how it seemed to make the world more real, colors more vivid against the monochrome backdrop. The killer wrapped his fingers tighter around the armrest of the bench, feeling the bite of the weathered wood beneath his gloves. There was something undeniably pure about the wretchedness of January, a clarity that came with the ice and the snow, a promise of renewal—or, for him, the opportunity to chase his macabre dream.

Women had always been at the core of his compulsion. They were muses and fears intertwined; they inspired both love and dread within him. From the moment "the frozen abyss" first came to him as a boy—a vision so clear and profound it haunted him—his fate had been sealed. Women would be his art, and their demise, his expression of how he felt about the world. But still, he felt that there was something else underneath the motivation, something he hadn't yet revealed to himself.

His eyes scanned the park once more, lingering on each figure, every breath visible in the frigid air. They were blissfully unaware of the predator in their midst, of the danger that sat so casually nearby. But he was patient, methodical. Today was for watching, for planning. Just as the artists captured the frozen scenes before them, he too would capture something—someone—to bring him closer to his icy ideal.

As the killers' thoughts spun, woven threads of anticipation and dread, the park remained oblivious to the storm brewing within him. The abyss called, its voice a siren song of frozen beauty—and he was all too eager to answer.

The park was an artwork of its own, splashes of color against the white backdrop of snow. The killer watched, his gaze sharp and calculating as the jovial group of artists attempted to imprison the winter scene onto their canvasses. There was something about their laughter, the camaraderie that knitted them together, which irritated him. They splattered paint carelessly, as if it were a game, while he knew that true art demanded something far more significant: it needed to feed on life itself.

Their ignorance was almost blasphemous. Didn't they understand that every stroke should be a tribute, an offering to something greater? Their vapid brushwork didn't create; it merely mimicked. He, on the other hand, believed in the sanctity of his work—a dark sacrament where life bled into death, where each kill brought him closer to the masterpiece he yearned to complete: The Perfect Frozen Abyss.

His eyes narrowed as the cold seeped through his coat, but he welcomed the chill—it was his accomplice, his muse. The park was an orchestra of muted winter sounds, but all he heard was the rhythm of his own heartbeat, drumming out a morbid anticipation for the act yet to unfold.

Rising from the bench, he approached the cluster of easels, feigning the casual interest of a passerby admiring their creations. One painting caught his attention, lying near the feet of a woman with hair the color of sunsets, so vibrant against the monochrome world around her. She had finished one canvas—a chilling depiction of snow twisting into angry visages—and was already coaxing another nightmare onto the second.

These were not the naïve imitations of her peers; these were visions that spoke to him. In the swirls of white and gray, he recognized a kindred spirit, someone who saw beyond the surface and dared to delve into the undergrowth. It was fitting, then, that she would be the one. She would become part of his gallery, her essence captured in a moment of eternal frost.

The killer felt a surge of twisted admiration for her, this artist who unwittingly mirrored the very evil that consumed him. His hands itched with the desire to begin his grim work, to mold her into the perfect piece for his collection, but he forced patience upon himself. Timing was everything when it came to creating a masterpiece.

As he lingered by her paintings, the woman with red hair rose and drifted away, leaving behind her unwitting contributions to his grotesque inspiration. The killer stood there a moment longer, committing every detail to memory—the way the faces in her art seemed to scream silently from the frameless page, how they too longed for release from their frozen prison. Soon, he promised them, soon.

The chill in the air was palpable as the woman with red hair left an empty easel to join the bustle around the food stand. The killer's gaze followed her, the steam from the hot beverages clouding around her like a shroud. He felt his heart quicken—not from the cold, but from the thrill of the hunt. She was perfect; she understood the depth of art that he craved to immortalize.

He turned to the artist beside him, a young man with paint splatters on his jacket and a carefree smile. The killer forced a benign expression, mirroring the casual demeanor of the others. "I'm sorry to interrupt," he started, feigning interest in the artwork spread out before them. "Do you know who painted this? I just can't seem to make out the signature."

The young man glanced at the canvas on the ground, where snow seemed to writhe in silent agony. "That's Zoe's work," he said, nodding towards the food stand. "Zoe Patel. She has quite a unique style, doesn't she?"

"Indeed," the killer replied, his voice steady despite the pulsing excitement within. "Quite unique."

Before he could steer the conversation further, another painter, this one older with eyes sharp as flints, peered closely at him. "Don't I know you?" he asked, the question laced with an edge of recognition that sent a jolt through the killer's nerves.

Quickly regaining composure, the killer offered a smooth smile. "Perhaps our paths have crossed," he conceded with careful nonchalance. "Art is a small world, after all. But I'll definitely keep an eye out for Zoe Patel's work in the future." His tone was light, but there was nothing light about the thoughts swirling in his head.

He turned away, heartbeat thudding against his ribs, not daring to look back at Zoe Patel as she rejoined the group, laughing softly, blissfully unaware of the fate he had crafted for her in the shadows of his mind. As he walked, the park transformed around him into a theater of macabre possibilities. Her body would be found at the outskirts of a treeline, her dark eyes staring into the void, a silent witness to the void he so cherished.

Snowflakes began their descent from the gray expanse above, each one a cold kiss upon the earth. A trace of a grin tugged at his lips, a private revelry in the knowledge that his grisly gallery would soon gain another masterpiece—Zoe Patel, frozen forever in his Perfect Abyss.

CHAPTER SIXTEEN

Present Day.

The cold lights in the Chicago Field Office buzzed with a low hum, casting a clinical pallor over the sea of metal filing cabinets. Carly stood at the epicenter, reading the labels with methodical precision. Gray was beside her, his posture suggesting an air of resigned patience as he watched her. They were both wanting another break in the case after Arthur Welling's alibi checked out.

And Carly had just found one.

"I'm certain this is a fourth victim. Zoe Patel, 1987," Carly murmured, drawing out a manila folder thickened with age and dust. The name didn't ring any bells for Gray, but he could see the gears turning in Carly's head. She flipped it open, and they both leaned in to read the details that had been buried for decades. "It looks like the others, she was most probably grabbed somewhere in Chicago, then taken to the spot where her body was found. Like the others, it was somewhere on the outskirts of the city."

"Anthropology student," she noted, "passionate, vibrant—it says here." Her finger traced the lines of text. Zoe had been full of life, dreams of digging through civilizations long past fueling her every step. Carly felt a pang of kinship; it was that same drive that propelled her own career, though their fields were worlds apart.

"Disappeared after a university lecture," Gray added, his voice betraying a hint of intrigue now. Timing was everything, and Zoe had vanished within the dark timeline bracketed by their other victims.

"Let's see what else we have on her," Carly said, flipping through the pages with reverence for the lost life they chronicled.

The room was silent save for the rustle of paper and the faint scratch of Carly's pen as she made notes. Zoe Patel's academic accolades filled paragraphs, painting a picture of a woman whose intellect was as radiant as her smile must have been. Carly imagined Zoe debating theories of human evolution, her laughter echoing in university hallways.

“Look at this,” Gray pointed to a photograph clipped to one of the reports. It was Zoe, her red hair and dark eyes alight with scholarly fervor amidst her cultural studies club. She’d been ambitious, aiming to reshape the understanding of ancient peoples.

“Another beautiful woman, snuffed out,” Carly muttered, the words like ice on her tongue. It all ended too soon—her body found positioned meticulously in front of a treeline, as if on display. Carly closed her eyes briefly, visualizing the scene.

“Whoever did this wanted them found like this,” Gray observed, his brow furrowed. “It’s not just about killing them; it’s about how they’re seen after death.”

“Why were these murders not flagged together as related?” Carly replied, her mind racing. The haunting image was a message from the killer, a signature that spanned years. Zoe Patel had become another piece of a macabre masterpiece that Carly was determined to unravel.

“Any number of reasons,” Gray answered. “Poor police work, possibly. But more likely, there was a spate of different murders in that era, and the police were stretched too thin to siphon through the deaths and see the patterns.”

Carly’s fingers felt the forensic report’s edges, crisp despite the years. Gray leaned over her shoulder, his presence a silent solidity as they absorbed the chilling details of Zoe Patel’s final moments. The words on the page were clinical, detached, but to Carly, they screamed a macabre melody that had become all too familiar.

“Look at this,” Carly murmured, tapping a finger against the coroner’s sketches. “The pose. It’s identical. And, like the others, he body had frozen over night.”

“Almost as if she’s sleeping in the snow,” Gray added, though there was no softness to the reality of it. All four victims had been found frozen, their limbs manipulated postmortem, arranged with an unsettling precision that had nothing to do with repose and everything with display.

“Her arms,” Carly continued, eyes tracing the outline of the drawing, “See how they’re positioned? As though she’s reaching out for something just beyond her grasp.”

“Same as Emily, Sarah, and Hannah,” Gray confirmed. The pattern didn’t just suggest a connection; it was a neon sign flashing in the night, pointing them down a path sprinkled with frost and dread. “It seems likely that the frozen winter is the reason there is a gap between kills. The frozen environment is a key component of the scene he’s setting. He had to wait for the right night to get what he wanted.”

Carly felt the killer's shadow in those photographs, a malevolent puppeteer arranging his lifeless marionettes. There was a signature here, one that spoke of a scene he wanted to recreate—a tableau etched in ice and preserved in the annals of unsolved horrors.

"Looks like she had something with her," Carly said, flipping through the case file until she came across a bag labeled 'Personal Effects'. Inside, amongst the remnants of Zoe's life, was a photo of a matchbook from The Velvet Room. She held it up to the light, the once-vibrant colors now faded.

Gray peered at the image, his face unreadable. "The Velvet Room? Another bar?"

"I remember mention of it," Carly said. "I think my aunt used to go there. It was another art-scene I think, but a bit more garish. My aunt always said the people who went there partied only one way: Hard."

"Looks like Zoe was part of that scene," Gray noted, thumbing open an attached note. "There was only one match left... Makes you wonder what kind of nights she spent there. Did she try to warm herself before her death? Or did the matches belong to the killer?"

Carly nodded, feeling the tickle of intrigue weave through her thoughts. The Velvet Room was more than a nightclub; it was a crossroads of lives and stories, where the anonymity of the crowd could cloak predator and prey alike. The matchbook was a tangible piece of Zoe's world, a whisper of music and laughter now silenced by the cold hand of death.

"Maybe Zoe wasn't the only one," Carly mused, her gaze locking with Gray's. "If this place was as popular as my aunt said, it's possible our killer was part of that scene too, hunting in plain sight."

"I knew your local connections would come in handy. Time to dust off those old club records," Gray said, already reaching for his coat. "Whoever frequented The Velvet Room back then—friends, lovers, strangers—any one of them could know something."

"Let's hope the owner knows something about that era," Carly replied, slipping the photo of the matchbook into her pocket. The clue was small, yet its implications loomed large in the silence between them.

"Wait..." Gray suddenly said, putting his coat down and rushing over to his desk.

"What is it?" Carly asked.

But Gray didn't answer. He seemed to be on a mission, oblivious to the world.

Carly strode across the linoleum floor with purpose as she crossed the office. She moved her chair and then slid into it beside Gray, who was already hunched over a computer screen that cast an eerie glow on his face. The clock on the wall ticked away the late hours, but fatigue was an adversary they refused to yield to.

"I knew it! Found something," Gray said without looking up.

"Hit me," Carly replied, leaning in closer.

"Sarah Jennings, it was mentioned in a throw away line by a friend," Gray explained. "Her movements were well documented. She had a pattern—every Thursday night like clockwork, she hit The Velvet Room." He spun the monitor towards her, a scanned image of an old credit card statement underlined in red digital ink.

"Consistent social habits make for easy prey," Carly murmured, tracing the lines of transactions with a fingertip. "Our killer knew where to find her; he could have been waiting, watching her there."

"Or maybe participating," Gray added. His eyes met hers, mirroring the dark pool of implications. "If he was part of the scene, he'd blend right in. Sarah Jennings was a fundraiser. It's likely she went there to meet with artists and other enthusiasts, building out her network of contacts in the art world."

Carly nodded, her mind whirring as pieces of the enigma started to interlock. The Velvet Room was more than just another lead—it was becoming the heart of their investigation. She felt the pull of the chase, the need to walk the same ground Sarah and Zoe once did, to breathe in the stale air of history and exhume its secrets.

"Zoe's matchbook, Sarah's Thursdays, it's more than coincidence," Carly said, sliding the cursor over the screen to open another window. Her voice was a steady drumbeat against the silence. "This place is the common denominator. They could have been chosen there."

"It's our best shot at finding a connection," Gray acknowledged, shutting down the terminal. "We need to figure out if our guy used The Velvet Room as a hunting ground."

"Which means we're going back to the eighties." Carly's tone held a grim determination as she stood up, reaching for her leather jacket. "And we start with every name that ever walked through those doors. Going by a quick search here, the club is long gone. But we could start with the owner at the time of the murders… There's a business record here of one Dominic Santos. He still owns the building and has a residential address near it."

"Then we pay him a visit before sleep," Gray said, finally standing up as well. "Hopefully, there will be a way to find old guest lists, employee records, anything that can speak for the dead."

"Good." Carly turned toward the door, her mind a storm of strategy and anticipation. "Because I have a feeling The Velvet Room will tell us exactly what kind of predator we're dealing with."

*

As they stepped out into the cool embrace of the Chicago night from their car, the city's beat seemed to thrum with the echoes of a bygone era, a time when The Velvet Room reigned supreme in the nightlife, and a killer might have danced among its revelers, cloaked in the shroud of anonymity. The task ahead was monumental, sifting through decades of dust and shadows, but Carly had never been one to shy away from the impossible, no matter how hard the climb.

Carly's footsteps against the pavement as she and Gray navigated the narrow, trash-strewn alleyway that snaked behind what used to be The Velvet Room. The nightclub had since morphed into a trendy organic grocery store, its sordid history buried beneath layers of wholesome paint and biodegradable packaging. But Carly could almost hear the imaginary echoes of bass thumps and laughter, the clink of glasses and the murmur of voices steeped in the decadence of the '80s.

"Should've been condemned," Gray muttered, scanning the modern façade with a critical eye.

"Maybe," Carly said, her gaze sharp, "but it's the people inside that make a place, not the other way around." Her mind was on the hunt, picturing the club-goers who might have rubbed elbows with a killer.

Gray heaved a sigh. "Let's hope the owner's got a better memory than this building."

They found themselves at the rear entrance of a dilapidated apartment complex nearby—the address of the former owner listed in public records. Carly led the way, the stairs groaning under their weight as they ascended to the third floor. She stopped at apartment 3B, the door a patchwork of peeling varnish and rusting metal. Before she could knock, it swung open, revealing a man of medium height, his dark hair now streaked with silver but his presence no less commanding.

"Dominic Santos?" Carly asked, meeting his piercing gaze head-on.

"Depends on who's asking," he replied, his voice gravelly, edged with caution.

"Agent Phoenix, FBI. This is my partner, Agent Grayson. We'd like to ask you a few questions about The Velvet Room."

The man's eyes narrowed slightly, but he stepped aside, granting them entry into his sanctuary. The apartment was an eclectic mix of retro memorabilia and modern minimalism. Vinyl records adorned one wall, while sleek, contemporary furniture occupied the living space.

"Retired life treating you well?" Gray remarked, taking in the surroundings.

"I ain't retired," the man said dryly. He settled into an armchair, every inch the king in his modest court. "So, what do Federal agents want with Mr. Santos?"

"Mr. Santos?" Gray said, eyebrows arched. "So you're not…"

"The names Carter, Danny Carter, I look after Mr. Santos's buildings around here," the man said. "You'll need an appointment to get an audience with Mr. Santos. And believe me, he'll surround himself with a ring of lawyers so thick, you won't even get a glance… So let me ask again, what is you're bothered about?"

"Four murdered women," Carly stated, pulling out her notebook. "Emily Rosario, Sarah Jennings, Hannah Grimes... and Zoe Patel. We know that Sarah and Zoe went to Santos's club, and it's possible the other two victims did, as well."

Recognition flickered in Carter's eyes, a fire reignited. "I remember the news, I worked for Mr. Santos even back then. Tragic what happened to them. But that was a lifetime ago. People came and went from The Velvet Room. It was the place to be. Bad things happen when there are enough people together."

"Any unusual occurrences around the time of the murders? Anything that stood out?" Carly prodded, watching him closely.

"Unusual?" He chuckled, a sound tinged with bitterness. "Every night was a circus. But if you're looking for monsters, there were plenty hiding behind masks of charm and cocaine."

"Was there anyone who might have taken an interest in these women? Someone who stood out?" Gray asked, his tone even.

Carter leaned forward, hands clasped, his eyes suddenly distant. "There was always someone looking for more than just a dance."

"Like who?" Carly pressed, sensing the veneer starting to crack.

"Names are easy to forget, Doll," Carter said, a haunted look crossing his features. "But faces... faces haunt you forever."

Carly felt the weight of years in his words, the burden of memories that refused to fade. Carter was more than just an old caretaker; he was a living archive of untold stories, and his boss could be a key to unlocking the shadows of the past. Carly knew that somewhere in the depths of those dark, reflective pools he called eyes, lay festering things sometimes best left undisturbed. And yet, she had to push on.

"Do you know if Mr. Santos would have any records of employees there, guest lists, that sort of thing?" Gray asked.

"Rat food by now," Santos said.

"Still, it would be good to have a look around the club," Carly said, knowingly. "It's just across the way."

"Mr. Santos leased it to a grocery place," the man replied.

"Yes," Carly replied. "But my research shows that the club was in the basement of the building, and there was a piece in a local newspaper recently where Mr. Santos allowed someone into it to take photos. Looked fascinating. The article said Mr. Santos was forced to keep it that way by the city, due to it being a piece of cultural history, dating back to the early 1900s."

Santos looked nervous. "Well…"

"We can get a warrant," Carly said. "And you can find yourself under suspicion for a string of murders that happened years ago… Or you can let us have a look down there, and we won't tell Mr. Santos. How does that sound?"

"Fine," he said. "Just don't disturb the grocery place above it. That customer pays his lease on time, and I don't want Mr. Santos to be billed for anything you law types break. It could be my neck."

He soon rummaged around in a box on top of a bookcase and provided a set of keys. Carly held them in her hand and felt they could unlock answers.

*

After moving through the closed grocery store and descending two flights of steps, Carly stood just inside the threshold of The Velvet Room, its long-closed doors creaking open like a crypt revealing its secrets. Carly thought back to her aunt's stories of youth gone wild and how the club kept all the original decor from a jazz club during prohibition. To Carly, she felt like they were trespassing on history, on hallowed ground where Chicago danced and boozed the night away for decades.

"Place smells like mothballs and broken dreams," Carly murmured, scanning the room through the beam of her flashlight. The worn dance floor lay silent beneath a layer of dust, the bar stripped down to wood and shadows. She could almost hear the reverberation of music and laughter, the clinking of glasses—echoes of life that once filled the void. It was here, amid the revelry, where Zoe Patel and Sarah Jennings' fates may have intertwined with a predator's desire.

“Let’s see if we can find any records,” Gray said, his voice steady as ever.

“You want to play music?” Carly joked.

“You know what kind of records I mean, Phoenix.”

Gray began a methodical search, his flashlight cutting through the darkness to land on forgotten corners and discarded relics.

Carly moved toward the DJ booth, her hands running along several vinyl records left behind. Each one was a potential witness to countless nights, and as she flipped through them, she wondered which tracks had played as Zoe and Sarah danced, unaware of the eyes that hunted them.

“Gray, look at this,” she called out, holding up a faded photograph wedged behind the turntable. It showed a group of people, arms around each other, smiling for a moment suspended in time. On the back, it said, 1988. “Zoe could be among them.”

“It doesn’t seem likely,” Gray said, joining her side. “But we can see if we can ID anyone in it.”

“Or if our killer was someone who liked being part of the scenery,” Carly added, sliding the photo into an evidence bag.

She felt a familiar tightening in her gut, the sensation of pieces falling into place but still missing the final puzzle piece. Every detail mattered—the overlooked flier for a themed night, the misplaced coaster with a faded logo, the lingering scent of spilled liquor soaked into the floorboards. This was a diorama of the past, and somewhere within it, secrets lay.

As they continued their search, Gray paused by a door marked ‘Private’. “We could be onto something.”

Carly stepped back to kick the door in, but Gray took the keys. The lock yielded easily to one of them, and they stepped into what once must have been Santos’ office. Here, the air felt colder, heavier, as though reluctant to share its secrets.

“Check this out,” Carly said, pointing to a wall lined with framed photographs. Santos was in several, always with a different entourage, his arm slung over shoulders, a king in his court. But his smile never reached his eyes, which looked out watchful, assessing.

“Someone like him knows everything that goes on under his roof,” Gray observed. “He’d know if a predator was circling. He would have known at least two people in his club were killed.”

“Question is, did he care?” Carly mused, her gaze fixed on Santos’ image. “Or was it just another night at The Velvet Room?”

They sifted through old receipts, reservation books, and letters, looking for any mention of Zoe or Sarah. Carly picked up a paperweight, a clear crystal orb that distorted the world when gazed through. It seemed a fitting metaphor for their case—clear yet obfuscated, each angle offering a different perspective but no clarity.

"Carly." Gray's voice broke her focus. He was holding up a ledger, its pages yellowed. "Look at this list of VIPs. Some names are circled."

"Regulars. Or maybe something more exclusive," Carly said, leaning in to study the page. "We should cross-reference these with the guest lists from those parties."

"Will do," Gray agreed, taking a photo of the page with his phone.

The investigation was like peeling an onion, each layer bringing them closer to tears—the kind that came from rage, frustration, or the raw pain of empathy for lives stolen. They worked in silence until their flashlights grew dim, and the chill of the nightclub seeped into their bones.

Finally, they had phones full of photos of records and notes jotted down. "We should see if any of these will help at the City Archives. We might be able to figure out who was here and how they connect to the deaths."

"The archives will be closed," Gray finally said, sighing wearily. "We've got enough to start digging in the morning. We can look into this Santos character."

"Agreed," Carly replied, though reluctance laced her tone. Leaving felt like turning their backs on the whispers that clung to the walls, the spectral traces of joy and sorrow.

They locked the door of The Velvet Room behind them, leaving it once again to its uneasy spirits. Outside, the night was quiet, Chicago a city of lights and secrets, with The Velvet Room as its dark, beating heart. Carly knew they were stepping out of a chapter of the story, but the narrative was far from over. Dominic Santos—and The Velvet Room—were more than mere backdrops; they were integral characters in a tale of horror that had claimed too many heroines already.

"Tomorrow's another day," Gray said, breaking the silence as they walked back to their car.

"But a day closer or further away from where we need to be?" Carly questioned, her mind already racing ahead to an uncertain destination.

CHAPTER SEVENTEEN

Carly wasn't surprised to find Gray already waiting at the austere lobby of the city archives building. This time, she had brought coffee for two.

"Thank you, Phoenix," he said. "Delightful."

Carly nodded, still tired, and then headed towards a room at the back where she could thrust herself into the work of going over what they had found at The Velvet Room.

Carly's fingers danced over the aged pages, the musty scent of history rising from the paper as she flipped through yet another ledger. Gray was at the neighboring table, his eyes scanning over the microfiche reader, lines of text flickering across his face in a steady rhythm. They were huddled in the dim corner of the city archives, a repository of secrets waiting to be unearthed.

"Look at this," Carly muttered, barely audible, yet loud enough for Gray's ears. She tapped on an article from the late '70s, its print faded but words still legible. "Dominic Santos—A Showman of the Night."

Gray glanced up, eyebrows raised in query before he joined her side. The article outlined a new bar opening, lauding Dominic as a local entrepreneur with the Midas touch, and a penchant for showboating. But as they sifted through more clippings, it became clear that Dominic's touch reached far beyond just bars and nightclubs.

"Laundromats, diners, even a bowling alley," Gray listed, his voice low and steady. "He's got his hands in every pie. Seems to spend most of his days at his restaurant, these days. It still has an active lease."

"Through business nous or fear?" Carly pondered aloud, her mind racing with possibilities. Dominic wasn't just a nightclub owner; he was a man who had woven himself into the very fabric of the community. It painted a more intricate picture than the simple suspect profile they had started with—a man who could be hiding in plain sight, shielded by his everyday enterprises.

"I'm starting to get a bad feeling about him," Carly's voice cut through the silence that had settled between them. They needed to dig deeper to see if the threads of Dominic's empire were stitched with darker deeds.

"Feelings aren't enough," Gray chastised Carly. "We need to be methodical. That's the only way to reveal the guilty."

Their search turned digital as they accessed the police databases. Carly's fingers flew over the keyboard, pulling up records, looking for any smudge on Dominic Santos' seemingly spotless past. Every click was a step down a corridor that grew increasingly narrow as they progressed.

"Nothing," Gray announced after hours sunk into the system. "No arrests, no charges. Not even a speeding ticket." His skepticism, a deep-seated part of him, seemed momentarily shaken by the lack of evidence.

"Too clean," Carly mused, leaning back in her chair and rubbing at tired eyes. A portrait of Dominic was taking shape, one with edges too smooth and corners too sharp. It didn't sit right with her—no one was without blemish, especially not someone with Dominic's level of involvement in a city stained with crime.

"Carter said last night that Santos would be difficult to question. Maybe it's time we stop playing by the book," Carly suggested, turning her gaze to Gray. His face was etched with the same frustration that gnawed at her, but she could see the hesitation there too, the adherence to the procedures that formed the backbone of his career.

"One must know which lines to cross," Gray conceded, a reluctant note in his voice. "What did you have in mind?"

"A little field work," she said, smiling. "Do you have a good suit?"

*

Carly adjusted the strap of her cross body bag as she and Michael Grayson walked into "Santos", Dominic's high-end restaurant nestled among the steel giants of downtown Chicago. The aroma of seared steak and rich sauces mingled with the clink of fine china, creating a sensory tapestry that felt at odds with their purpose.

"Remember, we're here to make the man feel uncomfortable," Carly whispered, sliding her sunglasses atop her head to better scan the room. She could feel the thrum of the city's heartbeat through the soles of her boots, each step deliberate as they navigated between tables draped in white linen.

Gray gave a nod, his eyes scrutinizing the clientele—sharp-suited businessmen, ladies who lunched, a flurry of waitstaff weaving through the maze with practiced ease.

They settled at a table with a view of the entire dining area.

"I want him to see us, to know we'll always be there when he looks around," Carly said.

Her gaze trailed over the sleek interior, the minimalist decor punctuated by bold art pieces—a stark contrast to the grime-tinged streets outside. This was Dominic's stage, and soon they would draw back the curtain.

"Two covers, midday, sir, ma'am," a waiter greeted them with a flourish of menus. They ordered something light, appetizers that wouldn't tie them down. Carly kept her eyes peeled for any sign of Dominic Santos moving through the space he commanded.

It wasn't long before they spotted him, threading through tables with an air of casual authority. Dominic was a silver fox amongst pups, his dark hair betraying only hints of gray at the temples. His charisma was palpable, even from a distance.

"Showtime," Carly murmured to Gray as she watched Dominic pause to share a laugh with a group of patrons. She felt the detective switch flick on within her, every sense sharpening.

"Let's hope he bites," Gray replied, his voice low.

With a mix of persuasion that hinted at urgency and the silent power of FBI credentials subtly displayed, they caught the attention of the maitre d'.

"Phoenix and Grayson, FBI," Carly said, quietly. "We need to see your boss. Tell him it's about The Velvet Room and four dead women."

The waiter soon disappeared from sight then returned, hastily.

"Mr. Santos will see you once he finishes with his current guests," they were informed, the words carrying the weight of favor. "Please, follow me."

The waiter led both agents to a small side room that seemed to be an old dressing room for entertainers.

Minutes ticked by, measured by the beating of Carly's heart. Finally, Dominic approached through the doorway, charm incarnate, gray-haired and black suited. He walked like a commanding storm, and his eyes pierced all who met them.

Carly's nerves sharpened—not from fear, but from anticipation.

"Agent Phoenix, Mr. Grayson, this seems highly irregular," he said. "I didn't know the FBI dealt with things in such an intrusive way."

"Carter told us you'd be hard to see," Carly said, pointedly. "So I thought an introduction, face to face, was merited."

Gray stood watching, his face serious and unmoving.

Santos smiled. His teeth white as a shark's. "I understand you have some questions regarding an old establishment of mine?" Dominic began, all smooth confidence as he took the seat opposite them. Carly noted the absence of sweat on his brow, the coolness of his demeanor.

"Yes, The Velvet Room," Carly said, her tone even, eyes locked on his. She watched for the micro expressions, the fleeting tells that might betray knowledge he wished to conceal. "We're particularly interested in the clientele from the late '80s. Zoe Patel, for instance."

The name hung between them, a test. Carly held her breath, searching Dominic's face for any crack in his polished armor.

Dominic Santos leaned back in his chair, the epitome of unruffled charm. His dark eyes, still sharp despite his years, fixed upon Carly with an amiable curiosity. With a practiced ease, he recounted the days when The Velvet Room was the heartbeat of Chicago's nightlife.

"Ah, those were vibrant times," he said, toying with the stem of a wine glass that caught the light just so. "People from all walks of life came through those doors. Lawyers, artists, students... Yes, even bright young things like your Zoe Patel. I remember her."

Carly's gaze didn't waver, studying Dominic's face as he spoke. She listened to the cadence of his voice, smooth as the jazz once played in his club, searching for dissonance. But Dominic was a song without missed notes, his narrative too slick, each anecdote gliding seamlessly into the next.

"Zoe was a brilliant spark, but you know, we saw so many faces. It's hard to remember specifics." He sighed, a masterful stroke of feigned regret. "I wish I could help more, Agent Phoenix. But if you trawl through anyone's life and question them over the death which they've seen, you will only find despair and… A waste of FBI resources."

"Several women are dead," Carly said. "I would think that required more empathy."

Santos leaned forwards. "Empathy is for the weak," he whispered, standing up.

Carly stood up and glared at the man. "Not as weak as a killer who preys on women."

"Are you accusing me of something, Agent Phoenix?" Santos asked.

"You're damn right!" Carly shouted.

Santos laughed, as if feeding on Carly's anger. "If you want an interview next time, please contact my lawyers."

Gray shifted beside her, a subtle cue that he too recognized the dead end they'd hit. They had hoped for a crack, a slip, anything to pry open the past Dominic held so tightly shut. Instead, they were left clutching at air, the scent of expensive cuisine mingling with frustration.

"Thank you for your time, Mr. Santos," Gray said, his tone polite but cool as he rose from their table. Carly stood there, arms folded, her expression etched with the resignation of an investigator who knew she had gone too far.

"We'll be seeing you," Carly said.

"I hope not," the man grinned, leaving the room.

"That man has crime written all over him," Gray said. "And of the organized variety."

"That doesn't mean he isn't the killer," Carly said.

"Agreed," Gray sighed. "But it makes it less likely. Our killer is doing this for personal reasons, Santos, if he's ever ordered a kill, would have it done over business. I'm sure of it. Nonetheless, a horrid character."

"Let's get out of here," Carly said, feeling dejected.

As they navigated through the maze of tables toward the exit, Carly's ears caught the hushed tones of discontent. A waitress, her apron cinched tight around her waist, was quietly seething to a colleague by the service station, unaware of the two FBI agents within earshot.

"...and then he cornered me in the wine cellar again," the waitress murmured, a tremor of anger in her voice. "I'm so tired of Dominic's 'hands-on' management. I know Jane left because she was scared of him, and I can see why. He's horrible."

The words clung to Carly like the chill off Lake Michigan—unwelcome and revealing. Something in the waitress's complaint snagged at her, catching on the edges of her intuition. She paused mid-step, exchanging a glance with Gray. Without a word, whole conversations passed between them in that look: suspicion, curiosity, the silent agreement that this small grievance might be a thread worth pulling.

"Keep walking," Carly murmured to Gray, just loud enough for him alone. "But remember her face. We'll check back on this later."

As they stepped out into the bustle of the city street, the restaurant door swinging shut behind them, the fragment of overheard conversation lingered, a morsel of possibility in a feast of uncertainties.

Carly's footsteps echoed slightly on the cracked sidewalk as she and Gray left Santos' behind. The restaurant's glass facade reflected the overcast sky, a distorted mirror of the city's dreary mood. She tucked her hands into the pockets of her coat, feeling the bite of the wind that whipped around the corners of buildings.

"Carly," Gray called, his voice steady but laden with concern. "Hold up."

She stopped, turned to face him. His eyes were narrowed, not in suspicion, but contemplation, the gears in his analytical mind turning. "We need to talk about this Dominic angle before we get back to the office," he said.

The unease that had settled over Carly since overhearing the waitress's complaint was gnawing at her insides. It wasn't just the words—it was the fear behind them, the kind of fear that spoke of power being abused, the kind that often accompanied men like Dominic Santos.

"Gray, there's something off about him," she insisted, her voice low. "I can feel it. And I know you don't like leading with your gut, but you have to know I don't rely on feelings without reason. I pick up things. It's why I'm good at what I do."

Gray sighed, adjusting his glasses. "I know you have good instincts, Phoenix, but instincts aren't evidence. We can't move against Santos based on a hunch and an overheard conversation about his character. We need concrete, actionable intel."

She nodded, though frustration simmered beneath her calm exterior. Her hands clenched in her pockets, longing for the weight of evidence she could hold, something tangible to justify the dread she felt. But all she had were the shadows that danced at the edge of her perception, taunting her.

Gray considered her for a moment, the lines of his face etched with the resignation of a seasoned investigator who knew when the trail had gone cold.

"I'm not saying he can't be involved," Gray said. "But you were this close to losing your head in there."

"I was simply applying pressure," Carly answered, but she knew that was a stretch.

"I think you should take a break for the rest of the afternoon," Gray said, gently. "Cool off."

"Don't be so condescending, Gray."

"Carly," he said, sterner. "I know what it's like to be swallowed up by these cold cases. All those deaths gone unanswered. All the grief the families must have felt. But the truth is, if you let that get the better of you, it will eat away at you. You won't sleep. You won't be able to think of anything else. And when you finally realize you've hit a wall you can't get over, you'll grow bitter. Trust me. I've done it all."

They walked in silence, the distance between them filled with the unspoken disagreement at the heart of their partnership. Carly glanced up at the looming buildings around them, the windows staring down like countless unblinking eyes, and wondered if somewhere behind those panes, wondered if the killer could see them running around aimlessly, laughing at them as they tried.

"Gray," Carly finally said as they walked through the city streets, the cold wind nipping at their faces. "Tell me about your first cold case. How far did you go to solve it?"

Gray glanced at her, his expression momentarily distant as memories stirred within him. "It was a case in Detroit, back when I was still new to cold cases," he started. "There was this suspect, elusive and slippery. I followed him for days, trying to get a lead. And then one night, frustrated with dead ends, I nearly broke into his home."

Carly raised an eyebrow, impressed by Gray's determination. "Breaking and entering? That's bold."

Gray shook his head. "Desperation makes a person do strange things sometimes. It was nearly the end of my career. My point is, sometimes you have to step back from a case and realize that you should step forward with care. If not, the ground might give way and swallow you up."

Carly paused, looking ahead at the bustling city before turning back to Gray with a determined gleam in her eyes. "I'm not going to break into anywhere," she stated firmly. "But what I want is for us to do some good old-fashioned police work. Wouldn't you have done that on your first case, if you could go back?"

"Yes."

"Well, let me check on a possible connection between Sarah Jennings and Santos," she said. "If I can show you that there is a direct connection between Santos and Sarah, will you let me put some more pressure on him? A little confrontation that could go a long way to helping the families of these murdered women?"

A smile tugged at the corner of Gray's lips as he nodded in agreement. "Perhaps I can do that."

CHAPTER EIGHTEEN

The cityscape dissolved into a backdrop of blurred lights as Carly and Gray sat in the unmarked sedan. Carly's eyes, the piercing blue that had stared down many a suspect, were now fixated on the entrance of Dominic Santos' apartment building. It was a monolith of steel and glass—a sharp contrast to the timeworn streets where their investigation had dragged them through the city's underbelly.

"We need to be careful with this Santos," Gray said, his voice steady despite the coiled tension between them. "He's a slippery customer."

"But we're now a step ahead of him with what we have," Carly replied, her words clipped with determination. She had indeed found a connection between Santos and the murdered women. And now she was going to use it to apply some pressure.

They exited the vehicle, moving with purpose toward the sleek structure. As they approached, she could feel the heft of her badge against her chest, its presence both a shield and a weapon.

They waited in the shadows, a strategic position that afforded them a clear view without being exposed. Time stretched, every minute amplifying the suspense that hung in the air like static before a storm. When the moment came, it was abrupt—a black sedan pulling up, its engine humming softly before cutting out abruptly.

Dominic Santos emerged, his figure imposing even from a distance. Dark hair, streaked with silver, caught the faint glow from the streetlights as he locked his car and began his approach to the building. Carly felt her muscles tense, ready to spring into action.

As they stepped into his path, Dominic's surprise was evident, but he recovered quickly, masking it with a bemused smile. The confrontation was silent at first, an exchange of looks heavy with unspoken challenges. Carly and Gray stood firm, their FBI badges revealed in the scant light, authority etched in their stance.

"Mr. Santos," Carly began, her tone even but assertive, "we have some questions for you."

"Agent Phoenix, again?" Dominic's voice, smooth and controlled, didn't betray a flicker of the anxiety she hoped to find. "And what brings the FBI to my doorstep this evening? Allow me to contact my lawyer and ensure it never happens again."

"Your nightclub, The Velvet Room—"

"Ah," he interjected, a knowing look crossing his features. "I suppose old haunts never fade away. You really are obsessed, aren't you?"

"Especially when they're linked to multiple homicides," Gray added, stepping up beside Carly. His presence was grounding, a reminder of the gravity of their quest for truth.

Dominic's initial amusement faded, his expression hardening as the weight of their inquiry settled upon him. The air thickened with tension, each participant acutely aware that this dance of questions and answers could tip the scales of the investigation.

"I don't know what you are trying to pull here," Santos said gravely. "But I'll have your jobs for harassment."

"And I'll have you in an interview room," Carly said. She took out a piece of paper from her pocket and displayed them to Dominic Santos.

He stood there in shock.

"This print out," Carly explained, "shows that you were at the fundraiser back at Fleetover Ltd., the night before Emily Rosario was murdered. It was organized by Sarah Jennings. That's a connection to three of our four victims. Now, we can do this in an interrogation room, or you can take us up to that swanky apartment away from prying eyes and let us ask you a few informal questions. It's your choice. "

Dominic Santos grinned like a wolf and let out a laugh. He leaned against the wall of his apartment building, his arms folded casually as if he were about to entertain old friends rather than being cornered by federal agents. "Murders? You flatter my humble enterprise," he quipped with a dismissive wave that seemed to brush away the gravity of their accusations like so much dust. "But let me put your minds at ease."

From within the confines of his tailored jacket, he produced an envelope, crisp and white. Carly watched carefully as he extracted several glossy photographs and handed them over.

"Since you asked about Zoe Patel earlier," he said. "I thought I should ensure that my alibi was verifiable. The images show me at *another* fundraiser, but in New York. I was there for three days, in the middle of which Zoe was murdered. You'll find printouts of receipts my accountant of 45 years gave me, as well as other documentation. Seems like you aren't the only one who prepares for things."

"An alibi," Gray muttered under his breath, his seasoned gaze scanning the photos before sharing a look with Carly. It was the kind of evidence that could carve doubt into the most steadfast conviction.

"Impeccable timing," Carly remarked, her voice steady but her mind racing. She turned the photos over in her hands, searching for any sign of forgery or manipulation—any indication that Dominic's alibi was anything less than ironclad.

"Courtesy of my assistant. I always make sure to document my travels, Agent Phoenix," Dominic said, his tone smooth as silk yet carrying an undertone of smug satisfaction. "I have done since I began my business empire. You're not the first FBI agent who has tried to pin something on me."

Gray cleared his throat, a subtle cue that signaled his momentary capitulation to the presented proof. Still, Carly's suspicions clawed at her, whispering that the facts were buried beneath a well-orchestrated veneer.

The city's nighttime movements filtered through air near Dominic's apartment, a backdrop of distant cars and muffled chatter that failed to distract Carly from the dissonance in her gut. While Gray examined the photos with meticulous attention to detail, Carly's thoughts churned with persistent skepticism.

"Convenient, isn't it?" Carly murmured, her gaze locked onto Dominic's dark eyes, which seemed to hold secrets deeper than the Chicago River. "You always photograph your meetings?"

"Only when they're important, Agent Phoenix." His reply slithered through the air, too slick, too rehearsed. Carly felt it in her bones—a hollowness that resonated with the echo of deceit. "It makes for a good press pack when needed."

"Your diligence is commendable," she conceded, though the compliment tasted like ash on her tongue. She watched him, the way he held himself, poised and unflinching. It was the composure of a man who had played this game before, who knew how to lay out his cards just so.

Carly looked at the photographs and papers. She felt in her gut that there was something off about them, an inconsistency that could be found to explain away Santos's alibi.

"Is something amiss?" Dominic asked, a slight tilt to his head, his expression feigning innocence. But Carly wasn't buying the charade. Her tenure with the FBI had honed her ability to sift through facades, to listen to the silent alarms that rang clear only to those willing to hear.

"You're sure these time stamps can be verified?" Carly pointed to the timestamp on one photo, her finger barely contacting the glossy surface. "Looks to me like they are a little off, this one says 2:36AM. That could get you to your destination *after* committing murder."

Santos laughed. "They are correct, and no, there are no discrepancies. I'm quite sure my alibi is airtight."

"Could be a difference in time zones," Gray suggested, but Carly shook her head. "That could give you some leeway with times."

"Or it could be Mr. Santos is more involved in this than he lets on," Carly countered, her words hanging in the air, a challenge laid bare for Dominic to refute. Her heart hammered in her chest, not with fear, but with the thrill of the hunt. Dominic might have provided an alibi, but Carly was far from conceding checkmate.

"I'm certain you'll find everything present and correct, Agent Phoenix," Dominic Santos declared with a self-assured smile, his dark eyes gleaming with a hint of challenge. "Feel free to verify my alibi to your heart's content. You'll see that I have nothing to hide."

His tone carried a veiled threat as he continued, "But let me make one thing clear. If I catch you or your partner prowling around my home again without cause, rest assured I have friends in the FBI who will make things very difficult for both of you." With a final nod, Santos turned on his heel and disappeared inside his apartment, leaving Carly and Gray standing on the dimly lit street.

Carly felt the weight of his warning settle uneasily in her gut, knowing that their encounter with Dominic Santos was far from over. As she exchanged a glance with Gray, she could sense the tension thickening in the air, a silent promise of challenges yet to come in their pursuit of the truth behind the chilling murders that haunted Chicago's past.

The chill of the evening seemed to seep into Carly's bones as she and Gray walked away from Dominic Santos' high-rise, the city's incessant hum a backdrop to their silent departure. Distaste lingered on her tongue, not entirely due to the metallic tang of the winter air. The neon glow of street signs cast long shadows on the pavement, mirroring the doubts that stretched through Carly's mind.

"Something's not right about Santos," Carly muttered, her breath clouding in the cold as she wrapped her coat tighter around herself. She glanced back at the imposing structure that housed Santos' apartment, its sharp angles cutting into the night sky.

"He wouldn't be so confident with his alibi if it weren't solid, Carly," Gray responded, his voice betraying a hint of weariness. "I'll get someone to check up on it, but this looks like it's going nowhere. We've got nothing on him."

"Solid alibi?" Carly paused, fixing Gray with an unyielding gaze. "Or manufactured? That timestamp discrepancy bothers me."

Gray's sigh was barely audible over the sound of distant traffic. "It's probably nothing. If he can show he was there earlier, it completely rules him out."

"Or he has a partner," Carly countered. "And Dominic Santos killed from afar."

"You're stretching," Gray said.

Carly felt frustrated at that, but she wouldn't let it go.

They reached their car, the government-issue sedan a nondescript presence against the curb. Carly slid behind the wheel, her fingers drumming on the steering column, each tap echoing her frustration.

"Without proof, we're just chasing shadows," Gray said, settling into the passenger seat. His profile was etched with resignation.

Carly started the engine, the rumble a tangible sign of progress, even if it was only to carry them away from another dead end. "I don't believe in coincidences, Gray," she said firmly. "Not in this job. He's connected to more than one victim, at least indirectly."

"Maybe," Gray said. "But the art scene from the 80s was a small community, it's not impossible that many people within it had connections to each other."

As they pulled away, the rear-view mirror held the reflection of Dominic Santos' building for a moment longer, a silent tombstone keeping its secrets shrouded in dirt.

"It's the only lead we have," Carly said. "We can't let it go, even if it's a long shot. Would you forgive yourself if we dismissed the possibility that he was behind the killings while secretly being guilty?"

"We'll go a little further," Gray suggested, turning to face Carly. He had always been methodical, a believer in the power of persistence and procedure. "But we should keep our eyes open for other possibilities."

Carly nodded, feeling the familiar stirrings of resolve. She maneuvered the car through the city streets, each turn taking them further from the glittering façade of Dominic Santos' alibi and closer to the heart of her stubbornness.

"You up for another late night? We could look at old employee records at the Velvet Rooms, see if we can…"

"Carly," Gray broke the stillness, his voice low, "we've been down every avenue for today. Maybe we need to consider—"

"That we're wasting time?" Carly turned to meet his gaze,

reflecting the city's glow like shards of glass. "I know, Gray. But my gut..."

"Your gut's been right before," he conceded, but his tone carried the weight of skepticism, honed by years of false leads and bitter outcomes. "But…"

"Instinct's all we have sometimes," Carly interrupted, her fingers drumming against the steering wheel. "We can't ignore it."

"Instinct and evidence have to line up, though," Gray reminded her, the words hanging between them, unyielding as the steel beams of the bridges spanning the Chicago River.

"Tomorrow can wait," she decided, her voice carrying a determination that felt almost defiant against the creeping tendrils of doubt. "We revisit everything, look for anything that might implicate Santos further. You game?"

Gray didn't respond, but she saw him nod, just barely, the motion more felt than seen. Together, they sat in the cocoon of the car, the city's pulse a distant rhythm against the quiet resolve taking root within Carly.

CHAPTER NINETEEN

The buzzzing lights cast long shadows across the walls of the field office, as if to underline the futility of Carly and Gray's endeavor. Dominic Santos, aged and bristling with indignation, had provided them nothing but smoke—a sleight of hand that left them grasping at air. An alibi that was almost too perfect, and no amount of digging that night had revealed anything more.

"Let's call it," Gray said, his voice carrying a weariness that seemed to seep into the very foundations of the building. Carly nodded, her thoughts a tangled mess since they had retreated from Santos' apartment. The man was a fortress; no crack in his demeanor had betrayed a connection to the string of murders that had kept Chicago on edge for decades.

"Another dead end," she muttered, not so much to Gray as to herself. Her mind raced back over the encounter, searching relentlessly for a misstep, a meaningful tell, a lapse in the armor of the former nightclub owner. But there was none, and the frustration simmered within her, threatening to boil over.

She paused by the exit, looking back at the web of offices and interrogation rooms where truths and lies danced together in a macabre ballet. The killer was out there, somewhere beyond these walls, a harvester of the living. And as the night staked its claim on the city, Carly felt the frigid grip of uncertainty tighten around her resolve.

The chill of the evening air greeted them as they stepped outside, an invisible barrier between the world of law enforcement and the city it sought to protect. Streetlights flickered to life, casting pools of illumination that fractured the encroaching night.

"Your resolve is admirable," Gray broke the silence, his voice unexpectedly firm. "Most would have given up by now."

Carly turned, surprised by the compliment. She saw respect there, in the lines that crinkled around his eyes, the set of his jaw. It was an acknowledgment she hadn't realized she needed until this very moment.

"But I see how disappointed you are," he said, softly. "I know it's difficult, but disappointment and frustration are part of the gig for a cold case detective."

"Thanks, Gray." She offered a half-smile, pushing a stray lock of blonde hair from her face. "I just... I can't let it go. This city, these people—they deserve answers."

Gray nodded. "I've seen agents come and go. They burn bright and fade fast. But you..." He paused, choosing his words carefully. "You see much of what others miss. You don't just look at what's in front of you; you look beyond."

His words were more than mere observation. They were a testament to her unique approach, one that had been chastised, as much as it had been celebrated, throughout her career. In Gray's eyes, though, in that moment, Carly saw something akin to validation.

"Coming from you, that means a lot," she replied honestly. There was a shared understanding between them, a silent agreement that they were in this together until the bitter end. Whatever lay ahead, whatever twisted paths they'd have to navigate, Carly knew Gray would be at her side.

"Let's get some rest," Gray suggested. "Tomorrow's another day, and we'll need clear heads."

"Agreed," Carly conceded, yet even as she walked alongside him, her mind continued to churn, piecing together the fragmented images and facts that danced just out of reach. The truth was there, somewhere in the shadows, waiting for them to shine a light upon it.

Carly's feet echoed on the concrete as she walked alongside Gray towards their cars. Their shadows stretched long and thin in the streetlights that sporadically illuminated the parking lot, a visual echo of the day's weariness. She could feel the cool air fill her lungs, crisp against the back of her throat, as the city's soundscape hummed around them—a drone of distant traffic and the occasional siren wailing into the night.

"Thanks for sticking it out with me today," Carly said, breaking the silence between them. Her gaze was fixed on the pavement, but she could feel Gray's eyes on her profile. "I know I might be a bit pushy sometimes."

"Partners look out for each other," he replied simply. "I've been accused of being too dispassionate. Perhaps we'll even each other out."

In that moment, with the sky a dark canopy above and the weight of unsolved crimes heavy on her mind, Carly felt a familiar flame flicker within her. It was more than duty; it was a call to those who had been silenced, a vow to speak for them when no one else would.

"Back at the BAU," she began, her voice steadier than she felt, "I thought I knew what it meant to chase monsters. But those cases... they were immediate, demanding everything of you all at once. Here, in the cold case unit, it's different." She glanced up at him, her expression reflecting uncertainty. "These files, they're like whispers from the grave. Each one is a chance to mend a fragment of the past."

Gray listened, his expression unreadable, but his silence was not one of indifference—it was the quiet respect of a fellow seeker of truths long buried.

"Every name we come across, every life taken—I feel them. And maybe it's because this city is part of my marrow, or maybe it's because these voices deserve to be heard after being lost in silence for so long. This is where I need to be, Gray. Whatever it takes, I'll find the answers they deserve."

She didn't see him nod, but she sensed his agreement, as palpable as the night air itself.

"I agree with all of that," he then said. "But I worry that deep down, you might be wanting to solve these cases in your home city because, in a way, you are trying to atone for something from your past. That type of emotional investment will not be good for you, if correct."

"It's not that," she answered. But the comment had made her uncomfortable. She knew there was truth in it. Carly had never healed the wounds with her brother Justin. She had never healed from the death of her mother. There was much she had to work through, and Carly could feel that was what drove her on.

As they reached their respective cars, Carly paused, her hand resting on the door handle. The lot was nearly deserted now, the cacophony of the day traded for a hushed stillness that seemed expectant, as though it held its breath for her next discovery.

"Good night, Gray," she said.

"Good night," Gray answered "Rest well."

Then Carly caught her reflection in her side window. For a moment, it was as though her mind presented her as one of the victims, standing there in a macabre pose. A statue of sorts, frozen in the elements…

A thought then struck her with the force of a revelation—a sudden, piercing clarity amidst the fog of fatigue. All at once, the pieces began to assemble themselves in her mind, not with the chaos of a jigsaw puzzle but with the precision of a sculptor chiseling away at marble to reveal the form within.

"Gray," she said, turning to face him, her eyes wide with the intensity of her realization. "The way the killer posed them... We know it's not random, not just about the kill. There's a deliberateness there, an attention to detail that goes beyond."

"Yes," he agreed.

Her mind raced, images of the crime scenes flashing before her eyes—the positioning of the bodies, the serene expressions, the unnatural stillness. Not merely death scenes, but exhibitions meticulously crafted.

"But what if it's like they're on display?" she continued, the words tumbling out as the epiphany took hold. "Each victim is posed with a purpose, almost artistically. We've guessed that he's not just a killer but a... a showman. Using their last moments to create a scene meant to be seen, meant to send a message."

"Old news, though, isn't it?" Gray asked with an eyebrow raised.

"But the bodies have been frozen solid by the cold," Carly said, excitedly. "We know he picks nights like that to kill, but what if there's more to it than that for the killer? What if he's making statues out of them!?"

Gray's face remained impassive, but Carly could see the gears turning behind his eyes as he considered her words. In that silent exchange, they both understood the gravity of her insight. It wasn't just the act of murder that drove their quarry; it was an exhibit of sorts.

"Let's revisit the evidence," Carly suggested, her voice low but firm, the spark of her renewed purpose igniting a path forward. "We need to look at the crime scenes again, but this time through the lens of not just an artist—or a madman's—final exhibition, but of a sculptor."

Gray nodded, a subtle shift in posture signaling his readiness to follow this new thread.

"This is interesting," he said. "It would keep us in the realm of art, but where the scene isn't as important, but the frozen aspect is. So, could he psychologically be trying to preserve something rather than recreate it?"

"I'll get the coffee!" Carly said, rushing back towards the office.

*

The city's murky light filtered through the blinds, casting long shadows across Carly's face as she leaned over the crime scene photos that were strewn haphazardly on her desk. The stillness of the surrounding office seemed to contract with each ragged breath she took, the air heavy with the scent of old paper and latent frustration.

"Look at their positioning, Gray," Carly said, her voice steady despite the whirlwind of thoughts churning in her mind. She pointed to a photograph where the victim lay, arms splayed out in an unnatural pose that suggested deliberation rather than the aftermath of violence. "It's precise—intentional. These women, they aren't just victims; they're his medium, and perhaps we've been paying too much attention to the treeline and similarities in the scene."

Gray stood beside her, arms folded, his expression unreadable. He had always been the one to toe the line, to follow the protocol, but Carly could see the slightest furrow in his brow—a hint of curiosity penetrating his skepticism.

"All this time we've been looking for a painter," Gray finally said, tilting his head as if trying to view the grisly scene from Carly's angle. "But the killer is deliberately making a sculpture of these women. But sculpture's are made to be seen?"

"Exactly." Carly's gaze didn't waver from the images. She felt a shift inside her, a pivot in understanding that sharpened her focus. "What bothers me is that if he's driven by a need for his statues to be found, then has he continued killing elsewhere and we just don't have a record of it here?"

Gray picked up another photograph, his eyes tracing the curve of the victim's arm, the way her fingers seemed to grasp at the void. It was a silent admission that her theory wasn't so far-fetched.

"It's rare for a serial killer to cease his crimes," he conceded, the word hanging between them like a tentative step over the edge of reason. "But not unheard of… This still doesn't answer the why behind his kills."

Carly drew in a deep breath, her mind racing. Each crime scene had felt like a puzzle piece, but now she imagined them interlocking in a ghastly gallery, each one contributing to a larger, sinister narrative.

"Control, maybe? Power?" she speculated. "Or perhaps it's about immortality—leaving a mark that lingers long after the blood dries. Sculptors often carve their works out of stone, wanting to be remembered for thousands of years."

"Immortality," Gray echoed. There was no mockery in his tone, only the dawning realization that they might be stepping into uncharted territory. That the profile they had been building was possibly missing a dimension, one that could lead them down a path they hadn't considered before.

"Let's take this from the top," he said, and Carly could hear the steel of determination in his voice. "We need to start looking for a sculptor, specifically."

Carly nodded, already reaching for another file. The night was pressing in, the gloom outside mirroring the unknown that they were staring into. But with Gray by her side, peering into the same void, she felt the flicker of an ember that refused to die—a spark of hope ready to ignite the chase once more.

Carly's fingers moved across the frayed edges of the case files, a rhythm born of urgency and newfound purpose. She and Gray had retreated to the bullpen, where the glow of desk lamps cast long shadows against the walls, guardians of their solitary quest. The room was silent but for the rustling of paper and the occasional muted click of a computer mouse as they sifted through the evidence once more.

"Look at this," Carly murmured, holding up a grainy black-and-white photo of Sarah Jennings' crime scene. The body was poised with an eerie grace, limbs arranged with deliberate care. "Every victim is positioned with their hands reaching out towards an empty space. But in one scene, we found the amphitheater. Could the killer be trying to connect his victims to his audience?"

Gray leaned over, his eyes tracing the contours of the macabre image. "You might be onto something. It's like he's framing them in a way. Like they are reaching out to the viewing audience, and he wants his work adored." His skepticism had given way to a cautious intrigue, the pieces of the puzzle clicking together in his methodical mind.

They pored over each photograph, each report, searching for the hallmarks of the killer's work. Carly's heart raced; the images before her were chilling, but the cold dread that typically accompanied them was now tempered by a fire kindled within her—a burning need to break the cipher of death laid out on these pages.

"Here," Gray said, tapping on a picture of Emily Rosario's resting place. "The skyline... it's framed perfectly behind the trees. And the entire environment of each kill is too similar… He chose these spots with intention, not just for the bodies, but for what surrounds them. He must have taken his time doing that, knowing where he would take them."

"Exactly. It's all part of his exhibition," Carly affirmed, her voice low but steady.

Carly typed at the keyboard with a purpose that mirrored the rhythmic hum of the precinct's late-night buzz. Screens cast a pallid light over the desk, bathing her workspace in an artificial glow as she pulled up case file after case file, the faces of victims staring back at her from a digital purgatory.

Gray rubbed his eyes.

"You can go home, if you like," Carly said, gently. "I'll stay a little longer and look through these old interviews of family and friends."

"For the sculptor?" Gray asked.

"Yes," Carly said, more determined than ever. "I'm convinced if we find a sculptor connected to the victims, we find our killer."

"And if you don't find that?" Gray asked.

"Then we look to see if there's another victim we don't yet know about."

CHAPTER TWENTY

Chicago, 1989

The night held its breath as Claire Thompson stepped out into the frigid embrace of December's chill. Her laughter, a melodious peal that soared above the murmur of departing theatergoers, played a haunting counterpoint to the sinister stillness around her.

From the recesses of an unlit doorway, the killer watched through eyes that saw not a person but a promise of what was to come. A form to be sculpted. She was alight with life, the very essence he yearned to capture and preserve in the macabre gallery of his making. She was the crescendo of his dark symphony, a note that would resonate long after her voice fell silent.

Her breath formed delicate clouds that dissipated into the night, a metaphor not lost on him; she was ephemeral, transient, and he was the force that would immortalize her. With every step she took, unaware of the fate that stalked her, she drew closer to becoming the final stroke in his chilling oeuvre.

Tension coiled within him, a spring wound tight with the desire to act, yet he tempered his urgency with the patience of a hunter. The moment had to be perfect, and perfection could not be rushed. His gaze never wavered from her retreating figure, his mind already embracing the cold splendor that would soon be revealed beneath the merciless scrutiny of the winter moon.

The midnight frost clung to the windows of the gallery, painting it in icy filigree. The gallery, a haven of silence and shadow, cradled the killers anticipation like a dark secret. Inside, the killer's hand hovered over a canvas that would never know the caress of his brush again. Instead, tonight's artistry required a different medium, one that thrived with life only to be stilled under his unyielding grasp.

The killer's breath was steady but quickened ever so subtly as he imagined Claire Thompson's form encased in ice, her brunette hair splayed like delicate tendrils within her crystalline coffin. In his mind's eye, she was already a masterpiece, her warmth captured in cold permanence. It was an act of preservation, a defiance against the decay of time and memory. He could almost feel the chill of her skin beneath his fingertips, the yielding of her flesh as he orchestrated her final performance.

Time was his accomplice, ticking away each second with meticulous indifference. The night had grown deep, the hour when dreams tread closest to nightmares. It was in this liminal space that the killer thrived, where the boundary between life and death blurred into his art.

Outside, the streets lay deserted, a concrete wilderness shrouded in the city's slumber. He watched from the shadows, his presence merely another unseen perspective among the alleys and byways of Chicago. His eyes, sharp as a falcon's, remained fixed on the stage door from which Claire would emerge—unaware, unwary, undeserving of the fate he had ordained for her.

The cold bit at him, but killer welcomed it, a lover's embrace heralding the consummation of his obsession. Each gust of wind whispered promises of the deed soon to be done, carrying away the remnants of his humanity with its arctic breath.

In his mind's theater, the scene unfolded with exactitude, each moment choreographed to fulfill the destiny he had carved out for them both. There was beauty in the precision, a perverse poetry in the premeditation. And as he stepped out, following the echo of Claire's laughter into the night, he felt the world narrow to a singular point of focus—the artist and his muse, the predator and his prey.

The crisp air hung heavy with the scent of impending snow, the cityscape a monochrome tableau under the gaze of the moon. It was as if everything had been drained of color, save for the vibrant life that still danced within Claire Thompson. Soon, even that brilliance would be muted, transformed under the killer's guiding hand.

Claire's laughter trailed off into the distance, a melody fading into the silence. And with it went the last vestiges of innocence that clung to the night. What was left was the stark reality of the hunt, the inevitability of the endgame that played out in the recesses of the killer's twisted psyche.

He moved with purpose, his steps silent against the frozen ground, each one a quiet declaration of the fate he was about to seal. In this dance macabre, he was both choreographer and lead, moving towards the denouement with grim resolve.

The killer knew the streets like the back of his hand, the knowledge etched into his being through years of walking them, hunting on them.

They were more than mere pathways; they were conduits to his darkest desires, allies in his quest for immortalization through death.

As Claire's figure receded into the darkness, the killer followed, his shadow stretching long and thin in the pale light, a harbinger of the doom that crept ever closer to her. This was his element, the stage upon which he performed his most intimate and grotesque of acts. Each step was measured, each breath calculated, each heartbeat a drumbeat counting down to the inescapable climax of his gruesome sonnet.

He was close now, so close he could almost reach out and touch the fabric of her coat, feel the lingering heat of her body that would soon be extinguished. The killer savored this proximity, the electric thrill of the imminent, the sweet tension before the pounce. It was a sensation he relished, a drug to which he was hopelessly addicted.

Yet, patience remained his creed. He would not rush this, would not allow the frenetic mania of his own excitement to mar the perfection of his artwork. Claire Thompson deserved that much—a flawless ending to the bright trajectory of her life. And as he stalked her through the night, the killer, the architect of frozen horrors, prepared to create his final and most exquisite piece.

CHAPTER TWENTY ONE

Carly felt the cold metal of her desk in the early morning sun, each tap of her finger echoing off the narrow walls of the Chicago Field Office. The stack of case files before her, a paper mausoleum for lives cut short and questions left to haunt the living, seemed to grow more oppressive by the minute. With a resigned breath, she plucked the file labeled "Thompson, Claire" from the apex of the pile.

"Gray, look at this." Her voice was steady, but beneath it ran a current of urgency that Gray, not long in work, responded to instantly. He approached, his eyes scanning the room with practiced caution before settling on the photograph clipped to the file.

Claire Thompson's face stared back at them, eyes bright with unfulfilled dreams and a smile that could have lit up any stage she graced. Carly felt a familiar twinge, the kind that came with the territory of cold cases—regret for being too late, anger at the senseless loss, and a relentless drive to unearth the truth.

"A theater performer," Gray noted, his brow furrowing as he read over Carly's shoulder. "And you think..."

"Look at her last known whereabouts," Carly interrupted, tapping a finger on the document. "She vanished after attending a play downtown. Intimately connected to the arts. It fits the pattern—public, yet strangely personal. She was chosen, Gray. I'm sure this is another victim."

The silence that followed was filled with the weight of implications, of pieces falling into place with an almost audible click. Carly leaned forward, perusing the text as if trying to draw secrets from the ink itself. Gray watched her, the initial resentment at their partnership giving way to a begrudging respect. She might dance on the edge of recklessness, but her mind was a scalpel slicing through the fog of years-old mysteries.

"Okay," he agreed, the word a promise to follow the trail wherever it led. "Have you got…"

"The autopsy report?" Cary finished with a grin, holding out a file.

The dim light of the office lamp cast long shadows across the autopsy report, the black-and-white photos stark against the beige tabletop. Carly traced the outline of Claire Thompson's final pose, her heart hammering a grim beat.

"An ice gallery," she murmured, half to herself, half to Gray. "He's not just killing them; he's displaying them. Like some sort of curator. That's his Achilles heel."

"Explain," Gray said, his voice low. He had seen enough death to last several lifetimes, yet the chill of this killer's method seemed to seep into his bones anew with each case.

"Each victim... they're found frozen, positioned. We both know it's too specific, too deliberate to be random," Carly explained, her mind racing as she pieced together the scenes of terror the killer had crafted. "It's also like he's preserving them, immortalizing them in death."

Gray leaned closer, examining the photo where Claire's body lay amidst a frozen landscape, her once vibrant features now still and pale. The artistry was perverse, a ghastly mimicry of the grace she once possessed in life.

"Whoever is doing this has an understanding of presentation, of how to evoke emotion through a scene," Carly stated, her fingers curling into fists. "But through all of that presentation, he's desperate to be known, to be seen. I can't help but think, if the killer is still around, that not only is he still creating statues, but that they are being displayed as we speak for all to see. This killer needs that adulation."

The realization settled between them, heavy and daunting. Yet Carly's resolve only hardened, her every instinct honed by the pursuit of monsters who lurked in the shadows of the past. She met Gray's gaze, and in that moment, they understood each other perfectly.

"Then we look for an active sculptor in the Chicago area," Gray said, the words a quiet vow. Together, they turned back to the files, to the frozen faces of women whose stories were not yet finished, whose silent lips Carly was determined to give voice to once more.

"Local artists, sculptors, anyone who might have crossed paths with our victims," Carly instructed, her gaze fixed on the screen where names and dates flickered by.

"Too many," Gray grumbled, frustration creeping into his voice. "All of our victims were somehow involved in the arts. They probably attended parties and places where every would be Chicago artist or sculptor frequented. We need to narrow it down. Look for patterns, exhibitions from the '80s, anything that ties back to the locations we know."

"Brilliant idea! Check for themes in their work. Ice, cold,

preservation," Carly suggested, her thoughts racing. "I wonder if the killer has even reproduced his kills as sculptures and no one noticed."

Moments passed as Gray stood hunched over his computer.

"Found something," Gray announced after what felt like an eternity. "A series of exhibitions focusing on the human form and the theme of ice as nature's great documentarian… Whatever that means… Looks like there are several artists in attendance that could fit our criteria."

"Let's see the list," Carly said, leaning over his shoulder to scan the names. Each one was a potential lead, a thread that they could pull to unravel the mystery that had eluded them thus far.

"Collective histories," she mused aloud. "Time to see where they intersect with our victims' lives."

Together, they dove into the depths of the archive, determined to emerge with the key that would unlock the chilling puzzle of the ice-bound gallery. Their search was methodical, exhaustive, fueled by the unspoken urgency that gripped them both—an urgency to restore names and stories to the women who had been reduced to artful corpses in a madman's collection.

As Carly sifted through another batch of clippings and photos, her fingers halted on a glossy brochure, the edge creased from frequent handling. It was an ad for an exhibition titled "Winter's Grace" dated back to the winter of 1986. The featured artist: Elliott Case. Her breath caught slightly as she studied the image—a sculpture of a woman, rendered in ice, every detail hauntingly lifelike. There was something unsettling in the figure's eternal stillness, a silent scream captured in frozen clarity.

"Gray, look at this." Carly passed the brochure to him, a frown etching deeper lines into her forehead. "Elliott Case. Is he on that list of yours?"

Gray leaned forward, his eyes narrowing behind the lenses of his glasses. He traced the outline of the sculpture with a finger, a grim expression taking over. "He is."

"This guy's work seems focused on ice themes," Carly replied, her mind already racing ahead. She didn't believe in coincidences, not in her line of work. "His sculptures capture people struggling. It's like he captures their last breath before it dissipates into the cold."

"From the database, it looks like he's still alive. Let's dig into his background," Gray said, reaching for his laptop. His keystrokes filled the otherwise silent room as Carly watched, her own heart thudding in anticipation.

The screen flickered with Elliott Case's history—accolades,

interviews, a list of exhibitions that matched the timeline of the murders. Carly's gaze was drawn to a photograph of the sculptor himself; those piercing dark eyes seemed to hold secrets darker than the depths of the frozen lakes his sculptures evoked.

"Got something else here," Gray muttered, scrolling through an article. "An old newspaper article on his work. Says Case prefers to work alone, late into the night, says it's when the 'true essence of ice reveals itself.' That's our time frame for each disappearance."

"Convenient," Carly mused. She could feel the pieces clicking into place, the portrait of a killer slowly coming into focus.

"Here's the kicker," Gray continued, "He had a studio in Old Town during the '80s. Not far from where Emily Rosario worked."

The revelation sent a shiver down Carly's spine. Proximity and thematic relevance—it was almost too much to be mere happenstance. They needed to approach this lead carefully; Carly knew that if Elliott Case was their man, he'd be cunning, possibly even expecting them.

"Gray, we need to bring him in," Carly stated firmly, her resolve hardening. "But let's play it close to the chest. If he's behind this, he won't go down without a fight."

"Agreed," Gray replied, already reaching for his phone. "No sense tipping him off before we have everything we need."

"Got an address?" Carly asked, excitement building in the pit of her stomach.

Gray looked grimly at Carly.

"What's wrong?" she asked.

"Look for yourself, Phoenix," Gray said, turning his computer screen towards her.

Carly's blood ran cold. Two photographs from one of Elliot Case's exhibitions were displayed. Two statues… And both looked almost identical to Emily Rosario and Claire Thompson.

CHAPTER TWENTY TWO

Carly's steps echoed in the cavernous space as she navigated through the shadows of Elliott Case's studio. The frosty breath of his sculptures seemed to mingle with the air, a chilling whisper against her skin. Gray, ever watchful, followed closely behind, eyes scanning the frozen figures that hovered like silent sentinels in the dim light.

"Mr. Case," Carly's voice sliced through the silence, commanding and clear, "Agent's Phoenix and Grayson, FBI. We need to talk about your work."

Elliott turned, his piercing dark eyes locking onto Carly's with an intensity that belied his calm exterior. His age was etched in the fine lines on his face, but there was a certain vitality to him, a stark contrast to the frozen forms surrounding them.

"Of course, Agent Phoenix," he replied, voice smooth as the ice he sculpted. "What can I do for the FBI today?"

Carly didn't miss a beat. "Your sculptures. If I were to look at all of them, wouldn't they bear an uncanny resemblance to victims from cold cases in the 1980s? Care to explain?"

Elliott's composure wavered only for a second before he collected himself, his gaze drifting over his creations. There was a reverence in the way he beheld them, as if they were more than just art.

"An artist finds inspiration in many places, Agent Phoenix." He spoke carefully, deliberately.

"Even in murder?" Gray interjected, his skepticism palpable even in the low lighting of the studio.

Elliott met Gray's gaze, unflinching. "Particularly in tragedy. Yes. I won't deny that."

The confession sent a jolt through Carly, her senses heightened by the revelation. It was a gut punch, the kind that made you want to look away, but Carly's eyes remained steadfastly on Elliott, searching for some flicker of guilt.

"Do the names Emily Rosario, Sarah Jennings, Zoe Patel, and Claire Thompson mean anything to you?" Carly asked, glaring at Elliot.

“Is that supposed to worry me?” Case said, almost arrogantly. “And what if they do?”

"Those women..." Carly started, her voice steady despite the turmoil brewing inside her, "they were someone's daughters, friends. Do you find beauty in their deaths? You certainly recreated their appearances in your statues."

Elliott’s hands spread out before him as if presenting his truth. “I’m not preserving death, Agent Phoenix, but I do what I do in the memory. Death is ugly—it’s final. But in ice, there’s something... timeless. I wanted to capture that.”

Gray made a small noise of disgust beside her, but Carly kept her focus on Elliott. There was horror in this admission, yes, but also a twisted sense of empathy that she hadn’t expected.

“Timeless,” Carly repeated, the word hanging between them like a verdict. “What’s timeless is that the families can’t get their loved ones back. That’s a timelessness that is an eternal prison sentence.”

“Exactly,” Elliott said, his voice almost a whisper, “A moment captured forever. Isn’t that what we all want? To be remembered?”

Carly felt a shiver run down her spine that had nothing to do with the cold. The room felt smaller suddenly, the sculptures too close. She wrapped her arms around herself, not for warmth, but for reassurance.

“Remembered,” Carly echoed again, softly. “But at what cost?”

Carly’s gaze didn’t waver as she absorbed the chilling justification of Elliott Case’s work. His studio, a frozen garden of human forms, seemed to leer at them with a thousand silent eyes. It was an unsettling communion of art and death.

“Mr. Case,” Carly said, her voice measured, “you’ve made your... fascination quite clear. But what we’re looking for is a connection beyond artistic inspiration.”

Elliott stood, his posture regal against the backdrop of his icy creations. “I can assure you, Agent Phoenix, my involvement with those poor souls ended when their obituaries caught my eye. I am an artist who channels the grief of this city into something palpable, not a murderer.”

His voice carried the resonance of someone used to declaring truths about his work, but Carly wasn’t buying it wholesale. She watched him closely, searching for the slip, the crack in the façade.

“Processing collective fear is one thing,” she pressed on, “but doesn’t it strike you as odd, Mr. Case, that your sculptures resonate so profoundly with the very victims of these crimes?”

“Art often mirrors life—and death—in ways that are

uncomfortable," Elliott replied, his eyes reflecting a cool defiance. "It's meant to provoke thought, to stir emotions. My work is a dialogue with eternity, not a confession of sins."

The air hung thick with his words, and Carly felt the press of cold, both real and metaphorical. The man before her was composed, his denial delivered with the smoothness of well-rehearsed lines. Yet, every syllable sculpted further doubt in her mind.

"Dialogue with eternity or not," Gray interjected, his skepticism hardening his features, "it doesn't exclude you from being part of this investigation. Your... intimate knowledge of these cases is more than a little troubling. Your fascination with the victims, even more so."

Gray stepped closer to one of the sculptures, his breath visible in the frigid air as he examined the likeness. "You see beauty where others see tragedy; it's a unique perspective—one that could easily make a murderer of you."

"Agent Grayson, isn't it?" Elliott turned his attention to Gray, studying him as one would a difficult piece of marble. "You think in terms of black and white, guilt and innocence. But life, like art, exists in shades of gray. No pun intended."

"Except life isn't frozen in place, and neither is accountability," Gray retorted sharply. "We're going to need you to come downtown, answer some questions where the temperature is more conducive to reality."

Elliott's lips curved into a thin smile, a crack in his otherwise serene demeanor. "If you insist, but I'm afraid you'll find my answers unchanged."

"You seem unperturbed by the possibility?" Carly asked, curious.

"Why should I be perturbed?" he laughed. "An innocent man should not fear false accusations."

Carly's gaze swept over the frozen figures that filled Elliott Case's studio. Each sculpture was a silent sentinel, captured in mid-motion, their glassy surfaces reflecting the scant light. Carly felt the hairs on her neck rise as she observed the details of each piece—too real, too familiar to be mere coincidence. She recognized several of the sculptures from recent national murder cases.

"Your work is haunting," she said quietly, stepping further into the cold domain, her breath misting before her. "I can see the pain etched into their faces, the stories they want to tell."

Elliott followed her gaze, nodding solemnly. "They were voices silenced too soon. I wanted to give them a chance to speak again, even if only through art."

Carly turned to look at him, her glare intense and scrutinizing. Jane Harper, Carly's mentor at the FBI, had always told her that the reality and evidence lay beneath layers of what seemed obvious. 'Trust your gut, Phoenix,' she would say. 'It's your most reliable tool.'

And Carly's intuition told her that Elliott was not their man. The connection between the sculptures and the victims was too overt, too brazen for a killer who had evaded capture for decades. No, this was something else—something more complex.

"Gray," Carly said, her voice steady, "I don't think detaining Elliott is the right move."

Gray turned sharply towards her, his skepticism an almost tangible thing between them.

"Based on what? A hunch?" he asked, his tone bordering on incredulous.

"More than that," Carly insisted. "It's about understanding the intricacies of human behavior. Not every dark inspiration leads to dark deeds. And my head and heart are telling me that while this might be macabre, it doesn't mean it's a confession. We need more, something concrete."

Gray studied her for a moment, weighing her conviction against his own doubts. Carly met his gaze without flinching, knowing full well the stakes of their gamble. They were walking a razor's edge, and it would take all her training and intuition to keep them from falling.

"Fine," Gray finally said, though his eyes still held reservations. "But we're keeping a close eye on him. Any slip-ups and he's ours."

"Agreed," Carly replied, sensing the fragile victory she'd just won. Her mentor's advice had steered her once again, but there was no triumph in it. Only the pressing weight of the riddle that still lay unsolved, its pieces scattered like shards of ice, waiting to be pieced together.

Carly's hand lingered on the doorknob, her fingers reluctant to release their grip on the cold metal that separated them from Elliott Case's studio. Her eyes met Gray's for a brief moment, an unspoken acknowledgment passing between them before she turned the handle and stepped into the crisp evening air.

"Mr. Case," Carly began, her voice steely despite the churn of her thoughts. "We may be back if anything else comes up in the investigation that requires your... expertise."

Elliott inclined his head, the ghost of a smile touching his lips. It was unsettling, that serene confidence he exuded, as if he were privy to some secret they could not fathom. The surrounding sculptures caught the dim light, shadows playing across the frozen faces, each one a silent sentinel to their departure.

"Art will always welcome scrutiny," Elliott said, his gaze following their retreat. "It is, after all, a mirror to our souls."

Carly felt Gray's presence at her side as they left the studio behind, the image of Elliott shrinking in the rear-view mirror like a figure in a fading dream. The sculptures remained, their chill beauty haunting the space long after the door had closed, sealing away the secrets they seemed to guard.

As Carly navigated the car through the winding streets, the city lights began to flicker on, casting kaleidoscopic reflections on the windshield. Gray sat beside her, a silent pillar of thoughtfulness, his mind undoubtedly turning over the pieces of the conversation they'd left behind. Carly could feel the unsolved case pressing against her, a palpable force that urged her to keep digging, to find the missing link hidden within the tangle of facts and conjecture.

She replayed Elliott's words in her head, dissecting them for meaning beyond the surface. There was something there, a thread so fine it was nearly invisible, but pulling at it could unravel more than just the mystery of the sculptures. Carly's intuition gnawed at her, whispering that they were stepping around the truth, circling it without closing in.

"Anything on your mind?" Gray asked, breaking the silence that had settled between them like a dense fog.

"Just thinking," Carly replied, her grip tightening on the steering wheel. "There's a piece we're not seeing. Something crucial that's staring us right in the face."

"Or maybe it's not," Gray countered, though his voice lacked its usual conviction. His gaze had drifted out the window, watching the cityscape roll by, lost in his own sea of doubts.

"Maybe," Carly conceded, though her gut told her otherwise. She drove on, the city's pulse syncopating with her own, both of them alive with hidden currents and unseen depths. As the stars emerged above, pinpricks of light in the darkening sky, Carly knew that more was to be revealed; waiting, biding its time, as all unfathomed mysteries do.

"Those sculptures," Gray began, breaking the silence again. "They're too close for comfort. It's like he's taunting us, or worse, showing off."

"Or mourning," Carly interjected softly, considering another angle. "Artists channel their emotions into their work; grief, pain, love. Maybe that's all it is for him—a way to cope."

Gray snorted, skepticism lacing his breath. "That's a poetic thought, Phoenix, but I've seen too many criminals hide behind the guise of 'artistic expression.' We can't afford to romanticize this."

"Romanticizing is not my style," Carly retorted, her gaze flicking to Gray before returning to the road. "But neither is tunnel vision. Elliott's connection to the victims is more than coincidence, yet it doesn't necessarily spell guilt."

"Instincts are valuable, sure," Gray conceded, the lines of his face hardening in the half-light. "But they don't stand up in court. We need evidence, hard facts, not feelings. I keep telling you this, but I'm beginning to think you're not listening."

"Understood," Carly replied, her words clipped. "But when the facts are scarce, we lean on what we have. And right now, my gut is telling me Case is not our man."

The car slipped into another stretch of silence, each detective ensnared in their own dungeon of thoughts. Carly felt the pull of the cold cases tugging at her, a deep urge to delve deeper, to piece together the fragmented lives of those lost souls whose stories ended in tragedy. Gray's desire for tangible proof clashed with her intuitive probing, creating a dynamic tension that propelled them forward, searching for the elusive truth.

The night had fully descended upon the city, cloaking it in a shroud of mystery. A chill crept into the car, seeping through the seams of the windows, an uninvited companion to their contemplation. Carly's eyes remained fixed ahead, the road unraveling like a dark ribbon, leading them back to the beginning—or perhaps, to a revelation that would change everything.

If Gray was going to push against her, Carly knew there was someone else she could turn to in order to crack the case.

CHAPTER TWENTY THREE

The office was a cavernous space that seemed to draw in the shadows as dusk settled over Chicago, and around Carly. Carly's desk was an island of case files scattered across it like flotsam. Alone now, with her partner Gray gone and the din of the day's investigation receding into silence, she reached for the phone. Her fingers moved over the keypad with the same precision she used when firing a round at the range.

"Jane Harper," the voice on the other end answered after two rings, its timbre carrying the weight of experience and unspoken understanding.

"Jane, it's Carly Phoenix," she replied, the formality of last names grounding her back to their shared history in the Bureau.

"Carly, good to hear your voice. How's Chicago treating you?" Jane's words held warmth, a balm to the sting of demotion still fresh in Carly's mind.

"Chicago is... it's home." Carly hesitated, twirling a pen between her fingers. The pleasantries felt like stepping stones over a chasm she needed to cross. "I could use some of that Harper wisdom right about now."

"Trouble with the cold case?" Jane inquired, her perception cutting through Carly's attempt at casual conversation.

"Something like that."

"Tell me about it." There was the sound of a chair creaking as Jane presumably settled in for the long haul, her attention focused despite the miles separating them.

"Have you ever heard of a killer creating sculptures from humans?" Carly leaned back, her gaze drifting to the window where the city's jagged skyline was painted in stark relief against the purple sky.

"Sadly, yes," Jane mused. "Several serial killers going back to Gein have tried with body parts. What does it have to do with your case?"

"Maybe everything, maybe nothing," Carly replied, frustration threading her tone. "It's not someone putting bodies together, but rather an artist type creating a scene over and over, allowing the bodies to freeze like sculptures. But each time I get close to something, it falls apart as a lead. It's like chasing shadows—every lead we follow, every connection we make, it just slips through our grasp."

"Shadows can be caught, Carly. You just need to shine the right light on them," Jane counseled, her confidence unshaken by the grim nature of the subject matter.

"Four women, all murdered back in the 80s," Carly began, her voice steady yet heavy with the weight of the unsolved crimes. "Three of them were stabbed precisely thirteen times each, a chilling consistency that speaks to a deliberate pattern. Their bodies were then left outside a treeline, positioned to face a large empty area as if... as if they were meant to witness something beyond their final moments." The details spilled from Carly's lips like shards of ice, each one sharper than the last as she recounted the haunting scenes that had etched themselves into her memory. Jane Harper listened intently on the other end, her silence a supportive backdrop to Carly's unraveling of the cold case's harrowing truths.

"Have you considered the significance of thirteen as a superstitious number?" Jane's voice, seasoned and calm, cut through the phone line, carrying a hint of intrigue.

Carly paused, her mind flickering over the details of the case like a slideshow of horrors. "I have," she admitted slowly, "but there are no other religious motifs at the crime scenes. No symbols or rituals that would point to any specific belief system."

Silence lingered for a moment before Jane responded thoughtfully, "True, but sometimes it's not about what's obvious. The absence of overt religious symbols could be just as telling. Perhaps this killer believes in something more personal—a twisted interpretation of faith or superstition that guides their actions."

Carly leaned forward, her gaze intense as she spoke into the phone, "Jane, I think all four victims are connected to the art world. The way they were posed, the precision of their wounds—it's like the killer is crafting a scene in his mind with each kill. It's not just about the murders; it's about the presentation, the display. Each victim becomes a piece in his twisted gallery."

She could almost see Jane nodding on the other end of the line, her mentor understanding the gravity of Carly's revelation. "It's as if he's curating a macabre exhibition," Jane's voice was laced with equal parts concern and intrigue. "The killer sees these women as more than just victims; they're his muses, his medium on which he paints his darkest fantasies?"

Carly's mind raced, connecting dots that seemed to form an ominous picture. "Exactly," she affirmed. "Each murder isn't just an act of violence; it's a performance, a statement. The way they were left out in the open, positioned with such deliberate care—it speaks to a meticulous mind, one that views these crimes as works of art rather than atrocities. But I feel as though if I can decode what the death scenes mean, I'll figure out who is behind them."

The conversation shifted then, as Carly delved into the specifics of her approach to the investigation. She detailed her methods, her theories, the meticulousness with which she parsed every piece of evidence. In the silent office, her voice became a rhythmic litany of facts and conjectures.

"Sounds like you've come a long way from the impulsive rookie I once partnered with," Jane observed with a chuckle that carried both pride and a hint of nostalgia.

Carly paused, the pen coming to a stop between her fingers. Those words, meant as a compliment, hammered home how much had changed. Gone were the days of reckless abandon, the leaps before looking that had marked her early career—and nearly cost her everything.

"Yeah," she admitted, a slow exhale pushing past her lips. "I guess I have changed. I had to. Recklessness doesn't make the world any better; it only brings more chaos. That's how I ended up here."

"Spoken like a true detective," Jane said approvingly. "Remember, evolution isn't just about survival—it's about becoming more adept at navigating the world around you."

She leaned back in her chair, eyes fixed on the notes scattered before her—each one a breadcrumb on the trail of a phantom from decades past. The Rosario case had led them to Jennings, then Grimes, and now Patel. Each woman's life snuffed out before their time, each crime scene a cryptic exhibition left behind by a meticulous artist of death.

"Give me some more of the pieces," Jane's voice crackled through the speaker, steady and patient. "What else connects them? Is there a profile?"

"Career women, all of them, with potential. They were... vibrant," Carly replied, sifting through the papers.

"So the killer may have insecurities, and he is wiping out women who are more successful than he is…" Jane's words were a reflection of Carly's thoughts.

"Yes."

“Carly, think beyond the physical. Beyond what you see,” Jane urged, her tone coaxing. "It's about the essence of these women, what they represented. A killer has a target for a reason, and the ambition angle may not be it, in this case. I would think that he is recreating death itself. But until you uncover new evidence, it's hard to tell."

“Thanks, Jane,” she said after a long pause, her words a whisper almost lost in the silence. “You’ve given me a lot to think about.”

“Anytime, Carly. You know where to find me.”

Carly’s gaze was fixed on the silent phone, its quietness echoing the stillness that had fallen over the killer’s trail. The abrupt end to the murders was a loose thread, fraying at the edges of her mind. She leaned back in her chair and considered the possibilities: incarceration for another crime, death, or a transformation so profound it acted as a full stop to the bloodshed. It was unlike a predator to just stop; they were driven by a need that seldom waned without cause.

“Or did you find another way to satisfy your hunger?” she murmured, flipping through the case file, eyes scanning for any hint of a shift in modus operandi. Carly had seen it before—a killer redirecting their compulsions into socially acceptable outlets. It was rare, but not impossible. As the lights hummed overhead, a shadow of doubt crept into her thoughts.

“Where did you go?” Carly spoke to the absent hunter, her question dissipating into the empty room. She turned her attention to the timeline, plotting the cessation of the killings against other events of the era.

“Ambition…” she said quietly. “We’re looking for a failed artist.”

The late ‘80s art scene bloomed on Carly’s computer screen like a forgotten garden, rich with vibrant history and long-dead aspirations. She immersed herself in the digital archives, seeking artists whose stars either rose meteorically or plummeted during the time the murders ceased. The smell of stale coffee lingered in the air as her eyes flicked from one entry to another—glamorous gallery openings, scathing critiques, interviews dripping with the hope of newfound fame, or the bitterness of failure.

“Come on,” Carly coaxed, as if the images and text could hear her plea. “Show me your secrets.”

She scanned old newspaper articles, some yellowed with age even in their digitized form, and found herself peering into the faces of young artists caught mid-laugh or mid-rant, their passion for their craft spilling off the pages. Their lives were a chaotic blend of color and shadow, much like the cases that lay scattered across her desk.

“Which one of you gave up the brush for the knife?” she whispered, fingers pausing over an interview with a particularly fiery painter who abruptly vanished from the scene. Her mind flared as she read between the lines of his last known statements—a mixture of frustration and resigned acceptance. There was something there, a clue to an altered life trajectory.

“Something made you change course,” Carly thought, the tick of the wall clock punctuating her realization. Each name, each face was another piece to consider, another angle to explore. “You… Became successful. Is it that simple?”

With this thought, she began searching, not for failures, but success stories. The last murder that she knew of was in 1989. From there, Carly began trawling through records for 1989 forward. She was looking for an artist, someone who hit the big time when the murders ceased. Someone who committed those terrible crimes, all born out of insecurity, and then stopped when they finally felt better about themselves. When they finally felt, they measured up.

Suddenly, an article came into view on her screen about a young Chicago artist named Adrian Bishop. And Carly felt like she was finally on the right track.

The article chronicling Adrian Bishop’s rise in the art world practically glowed on Carly’s computer screen, a beacon of transformation amidst the dim digital archives. The struggling artist, once haunted by failures and rejections, had found success as a curator at a prestigious gallery in 1990. His words echoed through the years, claiming that his struggles had been worth it, hinting at a newfound sense of fulfillment.

Carly’s mind raced as she connected the dots. A curator—a position that involved selecting, arranging, and displaying artwork for public view. It made perfect sense. The killer wasn’t just leaving his victims out in the open; he was showcasing them, immortalizing their beauty in death just as an artist would with their masterpiece. When he was finally given a legitimate place to do that, there was no longer a burning need to kill and frame his art with bodies.

As far as Carly could tell, there were no more killings after Bishop was made a curator. The killer no longer had that abhorrent itch. Another terrible thought crossed Carly’s mind, that Zoe Patel was the final victim because, in the killer’s mind, he had finally perfected his painting.

“Adrian Bishop,” Carly murmured to herself, the name heavy with implication. “You traded your benign art for something far more violent. Then you returned to harmless art when the opportunity to be a success finally came."

Her fingers danced over the keyboard as she delved deeper into Bishop's past, uncovering snippets of his artistic journey intertwined with the timeline of the murders' cessation. The pieces were aligning like stars in a constellation unknown to all but her.

As she read about Bishop's transition from struggling artist to respected curator, Carly couldn't shake the feeling that she was onto something monumental. The killer had found success after 1989, a turning point that coincided eerily with the end of his macabre displays. In the article, he even mentioned working as a truck driver to make ends meet. That put him right in line for the first victim.

"He stopped killing because he found what he was looking for," Carly concluded aloud, her voice cutting through the quiet office like a blade. "Recognition, validation... power."

The realization settled over her like a shroud of ice as she stared at Bishop's photo on the screen—his salt-and-pepper hair and sharp features now etched with suspicion rather than mere accomplishment.

Then, more searches. Looking into Bishop's background. And there it was, a picture in a local newspaper where he had attended a fundraiser where Emily Rosario's work had been showcased, no doubt by Sarah Jennings. Further still, Carly rushed over to Gray's empty desk in the dimness, switching on his desk lamp. She held the paper in her hand—the class roll from Eagle college art department. Bishop had been a student there at the same time as Hannah Grimes.

Finally, a search for Bishop's artwork revealed a horrid sight: A picture entitled The Perfect Frozen Abyss. A woman lay dead on the snow in front of a treeline, and before her lifeless body, was a perilous, chasm.

"Gotcha," she said softly, a spark of triumph lighting her face as a connection formed.

CHAPTER TWENTY FOUR

Carly stepped over the threshold of Adrian Bishop's gallery, ready for anything. Night was all around, and yet one figure remained at Picman's Gallery.

The space was a cavern of creativity, walls adorned with framed works that bled color and emotion into the sterile air. Hushed whispers from patrons swirled around her like echoes of conversations past, creating a haunting soundtrack to the stage that had been unwittingly set.

Bishop stood in the epicenter, the eye of a potential storm, an island amongst his own creation—a curator of beauty and secrets. Lean and athletic for his age, he was clothed in tasteful austerity, leaning intently towards a pair of onlookers, gesturing towards an abstract piece as if conferring wisdom upon disciples.

Carly's observations, sharp and unyielding, interpreted his performance. She knew the truth that lurked beneath his cultivated facade—the monster cloaked in a veil of artistic expression. Her heart drummed a rhythm of impending reckoning as she navigated the room, closing the distance between predator and prey.

She had messaged Gray, but she couldn't wait around. She had to see if Adrian Bishop was the man behind the murders.

With the precision of a seasoned agent, Carly intercepted Bishop's orbit, stepping into his line of sight with an unspoken challenge. There was no preamble to her confrontation, no courteous introduction to temper the blow.

"Adrian Bishop," she said, her voice cutting through the ambient noise with steely calm.

"Yes?" the man said calmly.

"My name is Agent Carly Phoenix with the FBI." She stared at him, looking for any sign of panic. There was none.

"How may I help you, Agent Phoenix?" he asked, tilting his head to the side. Above, a spotlight illuminated his gray hair, making his features more pointed and menacing.

"Working late," Carly said. "Glad I caught you."

“This gallery is my life’s work,” Bishop said, smiling. “It is my obsession. It even contains some of my own paintings and sculptures, so I am here night and day tending to it like a garden.”

“Painting and sculptures?” Carly smirked to herself. “That figures.”

“Why are you here?” Bishop asked, his eyes trained upon her.

“I believe you’re connected to the murders of Emily Rosario, Sarah Jennings, Hannah Grimes, Zoe Patel, and Claire Thompson.”

The words landed with the force of a gavel, silencing their immediate surroundings. Bishop’s salt-and-pepper brows lifted in feigned surprise, his thin lips parting to exhale a breath he’d seemingly been holding.

“Agent Phoenix,” he began, his voice a rehearsed melody of innocence. “I assure you, there must be some mistake—”

“Save it,” Carly interjected, her gaze unwavering. “I can connect most of the victims to you.” Her accusations were precise, each syllable a nail in the coffin she was erecting for him.

Bishop’s Adam’s apple bobbed, a telltale ripple of distress as he cast a quick glance towards the other patrons. Carly noted the movement, reading his desire for escape in the subtle shift of his posture.

"Every one of those women came into contact with you," she continued, undeterred by his attempts at composure. "And you even created a painting, The Perfect Frozen Abyss, which was dated 1984, before the murders happened. A painting that eerily resembles the crime scenes for all four women.”

Bishop’s hands, once graceful conductors of conversation, now betrayed him, quivering ever so slightly at his sides. But still, he held onto his facade, a master of illusion until the very end.

“Agent Phoenix, I’m an artist and a curator,” he said with practiced nonchalance, though his voice lacked its earlier confidence. “Not a killer.”

“Maybe you’re not a killer now,” she said, anger at the back of her throat. “But I’m quite certain you were once. Insecurity. Failing to be a successful artist. You couldn’t accept the world like that. And… The women… You hated them so much for being successful, you just had to snuff them out. All the while making your art. A deadly painting for some unknown fantasy, composed of those poor women’s corpses.

Carly stood before Adrian Bishop, the air between them charged with an electricity that could make the fine hairs on one’s neck stand to attention. The gallery was a stage, and they were actors in a play where the final act was unscripted, unpredictable. Carly leaned forward slightly, her attention sharpened as she continued her interrogation.

Bishop shifted his weight, the corner of his eye twitching almost imperceptibly. "You can't prove anything. That sounds like long ago," he stumbled over his words, a crack in the once smooth veneer of his defense.

"Art lives forever, Mr. Bishop," Carly retorted coolly, "and so do the wounds you caused the victims' families."

She watched him closely, saw the slight tremor in his hands, the way his gaze flitted to the door and then quickly away, as if betraying his thoughts of flight would condemn him further.

"Would you care to deny your involvement again?" she prodded, moving a step closer, her presence enveloping the room like a fog rolling in from the lake.

"Agent Phoenix," Bishop stammered, his composure fraying at the edges, "I've been an upstanding member of the art community for years. My reputation—"

"Is not on trial here," Carly cut him off. His desperation was palpable now, filling the space around them like the heavy scent of oil paint.

She took a moment to let the silence hang, watching as Bishop's eyes darted desperately around the gallery, landing on the shadows, the artworks, the exit, anywhere but on her. It was clear—Adrian Bishop was searching for a lifeline in an ocean where none existed.

And then, as if drawn by an invisible thread, Carly's glance swept across the gallery and settled on a piece of art that seemed almost inconsequential amidst the grandeur of its companions. A painting hung modestly to the side, depicting a woman's body sprawled next to a treeline, the backdrop a sheer cliff edge, all rendered in hues that spoke of both beauty and desolation.

Her breath caught in her throat as she read the title plate again - "The Perfect Frozen Abyss"—the words echoing in her mind like a dirge.

"And there it is!" she pointed with certainty.

Each detail of the painting mirrored the crime scenes too closely for coincidence; it was as though the killer had poured himself into the frame, immortalizing his grotesque handiwork.

"Interesting choice for a title," Carly mused aloud, never taking her eyes off the painting. Her heart raced with the realization that she was staring at a confession masquerading as art. She thought back to what Jane Harper had said about the killer's motivation. "It suggests a certain... familiarity with the subject matter. But what were you trying to capture? Something that happened to you, perhaps?"

Bishop followed her gaze, and Carly saw the color drain from his face, as though someone had turned down the dimmer switch on his life force. He wet his lips, and when he spoke, his voice was a shadow of its former self.

"Art is... interpretive. It's meant to evoke feeling, not to be taken literally. There is no murder scene, Agent."

"Of course," Carly replied, her tone soft but laden with implication. "But sometimes, Mr. Bishop, art imitates life a little too closely. And sometimes, life demands accountability for art that goes beyond the edges of the frame."

The painting, in its silent testimony, had just become the most damning exhibit in Carly's case against Adrian Bishop.

Carly's eyes were sharp as she closed the distance between herself and Adrian Bishop. The gallery was a silent arena, artworks witnesses to the confrontation about to unfold. Her voice cut through the stillness, each word a pointed blade.

"Adrian, you want to talk about your work?" Carly began, her blue gaze unyielding as she gestured toward the painting that had so deeply unsettled her. She knew she needed more to arrest him. "The Perfect Frozen Abyss" seemed to hold more than just paint; it was a window into a haunted psyche.

Bishop eyed her warily, his sharp features tightening as he swallowed the lump in his throat. He sensed the trap but played along, a cornered animal feigning ignorance.

"Ah, yes. A haunting image, isn't it? I… I have no idea where the image came from. It's always stayed with me… The woman… The treeline… The abyss…"

"Evocative," Carly echoed, her tone deliberate. "I suppose that would be a good word for it." She stepped closer to him, invading his personal space with her presence. "You see, I have a theory, Adrian. This isn't just art. This is your obsession laid bare—a moment you've tried to capture, one that's been eating at you for years. One that, when your career failed, you had to bring to life."

His expression faltered, the mask slipping as she pressed on. "This painting, these murders—they're all connected to something you can't let go of. What happened, Adrian? What's this 'perfect abyss' you're so desperate to keep frozen?"

Sweat beaded on Bishop's brow, his salt-and-pepper hair no longer a mark of distinguished age but of a life shadowed by dark secrets. Carly watched as the fear took hold, his hands trembling imperceptibly at his sides.

"Agent Phoenix, I believe you're mistaken," he managed to choke out, though his words lacked conviction. "I own the gallery, but I don't control the artists' expressions or their demons. That happens through the brush, and it remains a mystery even to me."

"Demons," Carly mused. "Yes, we all have them. But most of us don't turn them into a macabre series of killings. You wanted to preserve beauty, didn't you, Adrian? To freeze it in time because it's something you felt you never possessed. But what is the secret of this image? Who was the *first* woman? The woman in the picture before your murders."

"I… I need a lawyer…"

"You need to confess," Carly snapped. "Who is the first woman!?"

As the realization that his darkest secrets were unraveling before him, Adrian Bishop's eyes darted to the back of the gallery. His chest rose and fell rapidly, each breath a gasp of desperation. Carly stood firm, her determination solidifying as she saw him breaking.

"Where are you going, Adrian?" she asked calmly, though she already knew the answer.

And then he bolted.

Adrian Bishop, the man who sought to capture beauty in death forever, now scrambled to escape the grip of his own mortality. His movements were frantic, his fear propelling him towards the gallery's rear exit like a gust of wind urging on a leaf destined to fall.

Carly was impressed by his athleticism, moving with the speed and power of someone half his age.

Carly remained fixed in place for a split second, watching as the killer made his move. Then, as if a starter's gun had gone off, Carly surged forward, her slight frame cutting through the air with purpose. She was close behind him, the chase not yet given up, her resolve burning brighter than ever.

But in the world of Adrian Bishop, art and consequence had finally collided, and the gallery's silence was shattered by the echo of his retreating footsteps.

The gallery's air, once stagnant with tension, now buzzed with the verve of a frenzied heartbeat. Carly, her every sense heightened, blazed through the maze of art that adorned Adrian Bishop's gallery.

How she wished she had backup. But this wasn't like her days with the BAU, chasing active serial killers, cold cases were at the bottom of the list when it came to resources.

Carly moved as fast as she could, knowing she had to take care of this herself.

Each painting and sculpture she passed—a blur of color and shadow—was a casualty of the pursuit. Her focus, laser-sharp on the fleeing figure of Bishop, allowed no room for the appreciation of aesthetics.

Her boots thudded against the polished floor, echoing off the high ceilings as she maneuvered around a bronze statue, nearly toppling it in her haste. The sound of Bishop's own flight was a fading drumbeat ahead of her. She couldn't let him escape; too much hinged on this moment, too many broken lives clamored for revenge from their silent graves. His lead was stretching; the back exit loomed like an open wound in the otherwise pristine architecture of the establishment.

"Stop!" she commanded, her voice slicing through the air, futile against the pounding of their feet. She hurdled over a fallen painting, its frame clattering indignantly behind her. There was a rawness to this chase, a stripped-down urgency that had little to do with protocol or procedure. It was personal—it was about resolution.

Bishop burst through the back door, light from the street outside momentarily engulfing his thin, athletic figure before he disappeared into the city's embrace.

Carly emerged seconds later, the daylight harsh against her eyes. The city roared around her, a nocturnal beast waiting to bite, and yet indifferent to the plight unfolding within its bones. She wove between pedestrians with agility, her gaze scanning for the salt-and-pepper hair among the sea of heads bobbing down the sidewalk.

Cars honked as she darted into the street, narrowly avoiding a taxi that screeched to a stop. "Watch it!" the driver yelled, muffled by the glass and steel that surrounded him. But Carly's attention was tethered to the figure of Bishop, now threading through the crowd with the desperation of a cornered animal.

She pushed harder, muscles burning, breath coming in sharp gasps that matched the rhythm of her heart. This was a chase she had run countless times in her mind, each hypothetical ending with handcuffs and a confession. Not today, she thought, not this time.

And then someone banged into her. A bottle smashed on the ground.

"Look what you did!?" a drunk man sneered.

Carly felt winded, losing precious seconds. She composed herself and kept going, giving it her all.

Yet even as determination hammered in her chest, Bishop's silhouette became less distinct, swallowed by the finger-like streets of Chicago. She watched helplessly as the gap between them grew, her quarry slipping away like smoke through her fingers.

Finally, Carly came to a standstill, the weight of frustration settling upon her shoulders. Her chest heaved as she tried to catch her breath, her hands resting on her knees. She looked up, scanning the horizon where Bishop had vanished—a ghost among the living.

“Damn you,” she hissed under her breath, a promise more than a curse.

For now, Adrian Bishop had evaded capture, but Carly knew the hunt was far from over. The city might have shielded him today, but she was relentless. As she straightened up, the cold fire of resolve rekindled within her gaze.

This wasn’t the end. It was merely the calm before the storm. She breathed the icy air, wondering what to do. Then, a hand touched her shoulder.

"You're not giving up, are you, Phoenix?" a voice said. It was Agent Michael Grayson.

“Gray…”

“Let’s get our man!”

With that, the two agents rushed along the street together in relentless pursuit of a killer who had remained hidden for decades.

CHAPTER TWENTY FIVE

Carly sprinted as fast as she could, her breaths coming in sharp bursts that cut through the frigid Chicago air. Streetlights flickered overhead, casting long, dancing shadows on the snow-laden streets as Adrian Bishop's figure darted ahead of her—a dark wraith in the winter night. Carly's observations remained fixed on him, every sense attuned to the chase. The city was a maze of icy alleys and stark buildings, but she knew it like the back of her hand.

"Phoenix, I think he's heading... North on Wabash!" Gray's voice crackled through her earpiece, his tone urgent yet controlled.

"Copy," she gasped out, veering onto Wabash Avenue where the wind howled, almost celebrating Bishop's desperate flight for freedom. But Carly wouldn't let him escape, not when they were so close to ending this nightmare.

The cold stung her face, each inhale searing her lungs, but she pushed harder. She could hear Gray's footsteps behind her, determined and steady. They were partners in this—no, more than that—they were the thin line between this monster and his next victim. Every icy patch on the pavement, every unexpected drift of snow was a treacherous obstacle, but Carly navigated them with a dancer's grace, her drive and insight merging into fluid motion.

Bishop glanced over his shoulder, his eyes wide with panic, and Carly felt a surge of adrenaline. He was scared, and he had reason to be. His gallery owner facade was shattered, revealing the predator beneath.

"I'm right behind him," she promised, rounding a corner where a gust of wind blasted sleet into her face, momentarily blinding her. She blinked away the sting, her stride never breaking. The chase was everything, the world reduced to the pounding of her heart and the target before her.

Carly's legs burned with the effort, but she welcomed the pain; it grounded her, sharpened her focus. They had been on Bishop's trail for blocks now, their breaths visible puffs of steam dissipating into the night.

“Keep going,” Gray encouraged. “We’re gaining on him.”

The words bolstered her resolve. Carly knew that in chases like these, it wasn’t just speed that mattered—it was willpower. And Carly had that in spades. Her demotion had brought her back to Chicago, back to unfinished family business, and she’d be damned if she let Adrian Bishop become another loose end in a city already tangled with them.

She saw Bishop slip on a patch of black ice and nearly lose his balance. A lesser agent might have smiled at the sight, but Carly only narrowed her eyes and prepared to capitalize on his misstep. She ran smarter, anticipating the icy patches before they appeared, each footfall a deliberate choice.

“Watch out,” Gray warned as they approached an intersection choked with late-night traffic. Carly acknowledged with a grunt, her gaze locked on Bishop as he weaved between cars like a vampire fleeing the light.

They crossed the street in a dangerous ballet, honking horns and screeching tires creating a cacophony around them. Yet Carly tuned it all out. There was only Bishop, the embodiment of a cold case turned inferno, the heat of which threatened to consume them all if they didn’t stop him here and now.

“Carly, left on Michigan Avenue!” Gray shouted, his voice a beacon guiding her through the disorienting tracks of urban canyons. She banked left, barely avoiding a collision with a taxi that skidded past, horn blaring its indignation.

“Almost there,” she whispered to herself, though Gray heard it too.

“Take him down, Phoenix,” Gray urged, his voice a mix of command and faith.

And Carly intended to do just that. Because in this relentless pursuit, failure was a luxury she couldn’t afford, not with the imagined pleas of victims whispering in the icy winds, urging her on.

Carly’s breath fogged the air as she darted down the alley. The icy ground was a treacherous adversary, but Carly’s familiarity with Chicago’s backstreets gave her an edge. She could almost feel the city’s soul bearing down on her, its rhythm guiding her as she rushed through the network of alleys and shortcuts.

Adrian Bishop’s footfalls echoed against the brick walls, his silhouette a fleeting wraith in the dim light. Carly’s mind worked like a seasoned hunter closing in on prey; she predicted his path, knew every turn before he took it. When Bishop veered left in a panic, Carly cut right. Her shortcut led her to the mouth of a narrow alley that she knew would trap him.

There was a tangible shift in the air as she rounded the corner. The alley lay ahead, a dead end illuminated by a flickering streetlamp. Bishop skidded to a halt, his shoulders rising and falling with ragged breaths. He turned slowly, the pointed features of his face contorted in defeat.

"End of the line, Bishop," Carly called out, her voice steady despite her pounding heart.

He looked at her, the whites of his eyes stark against the shadows. There was no way out, no more tricks to play. Dressed in her black FBI jacket, Carly was an embodiment of retribution, the tip of the spear he could not evade.

He lunged a towards her, but Carly fired a warning shot, cracking the side walk at his feet.

Eyes wide with fear, Bishop put his hands up.

"Adrian Bishop, you're under arrest for the murders of Emily Rosario, Sarah Jennings, Hannah Grimes, Zoe Patel, and Claire Thompson." As she read him his rights, the words felt like a solemn oath to the lives he'd stolen.

With her cuffs locked around his wrists, Carly led Bishop out of the alley. The city seemed to sigh in relief, its chilly embrace a silent partner in their victory.

Gray appeared, out of breath. "You got him!"

"*We* did," Carly replied.

But Carly knew it wasn't over. She knew that more evidence was required to charge the man with the murders. But something in the gallery had occurred to her, a thread in Bishop's life she could pull, one that might very well lead to a confession.

If her instincts were right.

CHAPTER TWENTY SIX

The interrogation room felt like a refrigerated vault, its walls painted with shadows that played tricks on the eyes. The overhead light buzzed—a dull, electric heartbeat in the otherwise silent space. Carly took her seat, her posture rigid with purpose, as she faced Adrian Bishop across the steel table. Her file felt heavy under her arm, saturated with the weight of secrets waiting to be unleashed.

Bishop sat opposite, his salt-and-pepper hair casting a halo in the harsh light, his drawn features etched with indifference. He was a man who had wrapped himself in the guise of normalcy, a gallery owner whose hands were skilled in framing beauty, not crafting demise. Yet, Carly's suspicions writhed like live wires beneath her skin, sensing the monster lurking beneath the man's unremarkable surface.

"Adrian Bishop," Carly began, her voice slicing through the silence, "we've been chasing ghosts for far too long." Her stare locked onto his, steely and unwavering. Gray, sitting beside her, offered a silent nod—his expression taut, every muscle primed for the confrontation ahead.

Bishop's response was a mere tilt of his head, a silent invitation to proceed.

Carly didn't miss a beat. She slid the first photograph across the table, the glossy surface reflecting the fluorescent glare. It was an image of a woman, vibrant and full of life, frozen in time before Bishop's morbid artistry claimed her. "Emily Rosario," she stated. "Last seen alive entering a truck, never to breathe freedom again."

Gray followed, placing a memento next to the photo—a trinket from a diner, a place where laughter once mingled with the aroma of coffee and pie. He added, "A waitress with dreams and hopes all of her own."

Witness statements fluttered down like fall leaves, each one a record of moments witnessed, words overheard, patterns recognized. They spoke of a man lurking in the shadows, of conversations cut short when he entered the room, of artistic aspirations curdled by constant rejection.

With each piece of evidence laid bare, Carly watched the stoic mask that Bishop wore begin to fracture. His fingers twitched atop the cold metal table, the only betrayal of the turmoil that Carly imagined churned within him. As the chain of culpability tightened link by indelible link, Bishop's eyes grew distant, retreating to a place where only he could hear the echoes of his own depravity.

"Your work speaks volumes, Mr. Bishop," Carly said, her tone edged with the chill of certainty. "But before you became a curator, it wasn't the kind found hanging in galleries. It's the kind that hangs heavy on the souls of those you've taken."

Bishop's Adam's apple bobbed in a swallow that seemed to carry the gravity of his crimes. For a fleeting moment, Carly wondered if she glimpsed the glint of fear—or was it surrender?—in his eyes. She pressed on, relentless, feeling the threads of the web they'd woven drawing tighter around their quarry.

"And then Sarah Jennings, Hannah Grimes, Zoe Patel..." Gray recited the names, each a solemn drumbeat in the dirge of Bishop's making. "All women who shone too brightly. All women are now silenced by your design."

The interrogation room became a crucible, the air charged with the imminent collapse of a façade decades in the making. Carly and Gray sat there, the seekers of truths that Adrian Bishop had thought buried in the quiet corners of the past. But the truth, as Carly knew all too well, was a specter that never tired of the hunt. And tonight, it had come calling for Adrian Bishop.

Carly's fingers were a steady metronome against the cold steel of the table, each tap a countdown to the moment she would fracture the world Adrian Bishop had built. She observed him, his eyes darting like captive birds seeking an escape that wasn't there. Carly knew the power of the right evidence at the right time—it was a conductor's baton, able to orchestrate a crescendo from the most silent of suspects.

"You don't have any proof of this!" he sniped. "I'll walk out of here free and easy, back to my gallery, and you and your sidekick here will be sickened with that thought for the rest of your careers."

Carly smiled. She had something up her sleeve that Bishop hadn't considered. Something only she herself had uncovered.

"Mr. Bishop," she began, voice low and controlled as she slid the file across the table. The manila folder parted like curtains on a stage, revealing its contents—a series of black and white photographs splayed out between them. In the grainy images, a woman lay prostrate, her form echoing the stark shapes of the trees behind her, a dark silhouette against the pale cliff edge.

"Not one of your victims... Ellen Bishop," she said, letting the name hang in the air. "1962." Each detail sharpened the focus on the scene—the way the victim's arm was bent, the unnatural angle of her head, the serene yet horrific stillness.

Bishop's façade crumbled, brick by brick, as if Carly's words were a mallet to his defenses. His complexion blanched, a stark contrast to the dark room, his breathing shallow and rapid. His gaze transfixed on the image of Ellen Bishop—his mother—as if seeing her for the first time. A truth he could no longer deny.

"Mom," he whispered, the syllable a dreaded sound deadened by the sterile room. Carly watched, clinical yet empathetic, as the fortress within which Adrian Bishop resided started to dissolve.

The silence was heavy, pregnant with the confession that hung on the edge of Bishop's lips. Carly leaned forward, her vision reflecting the glow above, piercing through the gloom. She waited, patient as a spider at the center of a web, for her prey to entangle itself further in the strands of their own making.

"Let me tell you about your 'artistic vision,' Mr. Bishop," she prompted softly, nudging him toward the precipice of revelation. "There was something that stuck in my mind this entire time. It was the *who*, not the *why* of it all. Who was the woman you were trying to capture for eternity in your works of art.

"At first, I thought you were killing the same woman over and over again. But then it hit me, you weren't. You were trying to preserve something. Freezing it for eternity. And that then led me to... Who were you trying to preserve? And so, I searched for trauma. *Your* trauma. Because that is where all killers are born."

Carly looked at the photograph again. Gray sat next to her saying nothing, only watching. He gave her a supportive nod that said *keep going*.

"Ellen Bishop..." Carly said, softly. "She was your mother. I found all the information on her in our archives. The irony is, her murder is a cold case. She was found in the winter of 1962. She had been strangled and stabbed. She was dumped on the treeline in front of a cliff. 'The Perfect Frozen Abyss' is like your painting.

"Please don't..." Bishop whispered.

"I read the police report," Carly said. "You were the one who found her. But you were only 4 years old."

"I don't remember..." he said, touching the photograph of his murdered mother.

"But it was in there," Carly explained. "All these years. It was there. Tell me, are you superstitious about the number 13?"

Bishop looked sick at that question. "How… How do you know that?"

"Because, Adrian," Carly said, leaning in. "The victims were stabbed 13 times. The same number as the date when you found your mom. The 13th of December, 1962."

Adrian Bishop's shoulders shook as he succumbed to a grief that seemed to claw its way out of his throat. His hands covered his face, and when they fell away, it was as if they pulled the mask off with them. Raw, unguarded emotion bled into the room.

"It was... all about capturing... the beauty," Bishop gasped between sobs, his voice breaking under the strain of his confession. "Her death—it was a... masterpiece, frozen in time."

He leaned forward, his tears spilling onto the photographs, as if trying to blur the lines between past and present. "My victims... they were... embodiments of her—her drive, her grace. I chose them because..." He trailed off, caught in the snare of his own twisted nostalgia.

"Because they reminded you of her," Carly finished, her tone not unkind but relentless in its pursuit of the truth. She felt the weight of years of investigation shifting, aligning into a picture of clarity and resolve.

"Ellen Bishop," she repeated, grounding herself in the reality of the name. "Your muse, your model, your mother." Her words were the finishing touches to a portrait long left incomplete, finally revealing the artist behind the crimson strokes.

Carly's eyes never left Adrian Bishop as he continued to unravel before them, his confession painting a grotesque picture of his shattered psyche. Each word he uttered was a maddening addition to his twisted reality. She watched him—the man who had been an enigmatic shadow in their case files, now reduced to a broken soul confessing to recreating the tableau of his mother's death through the lives of innocent women.

"Every detail... it had to be perfect," Bishop whispered, his voice a hollow echo of the gallery owner who once spoke passionately about art and beauty. "The light, the pose, the fear in their eyes—it was the only way I could feel close to her again."

Gray shifted uncomfortably beside Carly, his hardened exterior crumbling at the horror of Bishop's admission. It was clear they were not just looking at a murderer; they were staring into the heart of a man whose life had been irrevocably entwined with death.

Carly felt the air thicken, her own breath catching as she absorbed the magnitude of Bishop's deranged pursuit. This was more than a case closed; it was a chilling reminder that the human mind could harbor depravity deeper than any crime scene suggested.

"Adrian," she probed gently, yet firmly, "you sought to immortalize your mother through the suffering of others. Why?"

"Because death is the ultimate art," he murmured, his gaze lost somewhere between remorse and madness. "It's eternal, unchanging—like her memory. But I didn't truly understand what I was doing. It was inside of me… Only now, since you came along…"

In the silence that followed, Carly realized that this insight into Bishop's mind was both an answer and a curse—a glimpse into a chasm no amount of justice could ever fill.

Bishop's words hung suspended in the stale air of the interrogation room, resonating with a finality that marked the end of the long, treacherous path Carly had walked. As Gray began the formalities of concluding their session, Carly allowed herself a moment to step back from the precipice they'd all been teetering on.

She stood up, her movements deliberate but heavy with the gravity of what they'd achieved. The cold fluorescence of the room seemed less oppressive now, its sterile light somehow softer around the edges. Carly glanced down at the file still clutched in her hands, the edges frayed from the countless times she'd opened it, searching for theories and evidence intertwined with years of dead ends and faded ink.

Carly looked at the pathetic figure before her. "Adrian Bishop, you are now being charged with the murders of Emily Rosario, Sarah Jennings, Hannah Grimes, Zoe Patel, and Claire Thompson. Someone will be with you to read you your rights."

Carly couldn't stand being in that room any longer, and so she left, her partner close behind her.

"Are you alright?" Gray's voice broke through her reverie, laden with a concern that transcended their professional bond.

Carly nodded. "I'm fine. Just thinking about the families... how they can finally start healing."

"Thanks to you," Gray added, his tone conveying respect that needed no embellishment. "I'll go and let our superiors know you've solved the case."

They locked eyes for a brief second, acknowledging the journey that had led them here—to this room, to Bishop's breakdown, to closure. Carly felt a swell of pride, not just for herself, but for the team, for the relentless pursuit that had brought them face-to-face with the abyss and allowed them to pull something back from it.

"In the morning," she said, her voice steady with newfound resolve. "We can finally tell the families it's all over."

As they walked in different directions, parting in the hallway of the Chicago Field Office, Carly knew that this case would leave its scars, a permanent etching on her career and soul. But for now, there was solace in knowing that the shadows she had chased had finally been illuminated by the light of truth, and the ghosts of the past could rest in peace.

Emotions began to overflow at the thought, and so Carly, not wishing to outwardly show them, disappeared into a small empty interview room and cried, before falling asleep exhausted in one of the chairs.

CHAPTER TWENTY SEVEN

Carly's fingers were still trembling from the adrenaline of the arrest as she stepped out of the precinct, her breath visible in the crisp Chicago air. It was early morning, the sky a tapestry of deep blues and purples that seemed to bleed into the cityscape. She pulled her coat tighter around her, more for comfort than warmth, and started towards her apartment.

Her phone buzzed, and she fished it out of her pocket with a sense of unease. It wasn't a number she recognized, but intuition nudged her to answer.

"Phoenix," she said, her voice steady despite the lingering rush of blood in her ears.

"Carly, it's Director Hargrove." The voice on the other end was unexpected, pulling her back to a world she had been forcibly ejected from months ago. Her former boss.

"Sir?" Carly's step faltered, the familiar tone igniting a spark of her past life within the Behavioral Analysis Unit.

"I'll cut to the chase. I just got off the phone with your partner, Agent Grayson. He called to say he thinks you deserve a commendation for solving the murder of five women… Incredible work. Look… I know it's a fast turnaround, but high profile news is just what you need to get your old job back. It's going to be a real good piece of PR for the Bureau, identifying and then apprehending a serial killer who took at least four lives. I'm impressed, and so are some of your other superiors.

"It's come to our attention that we might have been a little hasty moving you over there to Chicago. We just lost another agent to retirement, and we could do with your talents again. We want you back at the BAU," he stated, his voice a mix of business and a softer edge she hadn't heard before.

The news should have sent waves of excitement through her, an opportunity to reclaim the position she'd lost. But now, the words settled oddly, tangled up with threads of doubt. Her days delving into cold cases had altered her, the slow and meticulous unraveling of long-forgotten stories resonating deeply with her own need to piece together the fragmented parts of herself.

"Sir, I—" Carly began, but a lump formed in her throat, cutting off the rest of her sentence.

"Think about it, Phoenix. You've got 48 hours," Lewis replied, leaving the line dead before she could protest.

Carly stood motionless, the dying light casting long shadows across the pavement. The once-coveted position within the BAU loomed over her like a specter of her former self, yet the silent whisper of cold cases beckoned, promising a fulfillment she'd only recently discovered.

She continued walking, each step carrying the weight of her thoughts. Her mind raced through the possibilities, the allure of returning to the BAU's fast-paced world of profiling and pursuit conflicting with the quiet satisfaction found in solving puzzles left untouched by time.

Her mind was awash with thoughts and feelings. Now that the case was solved, there was only one place she wanted to go to, a place she had avoided so far since returning to Chicago a few days earlier.

*

Carly stepped out of her car, the crunch of gravel beneath her feet punctuating the stillness of the cemetery. Row upon row of headstones marched in somber silence, their shadows stretching long and thin as the sun dipped low, painting the horizon in hues of fading gold and bruised purple. She moved with quiet purpose, her heart a metronome ticking away the moments as she approached the grave that had called to her across the years.

The grass whispered against her pants as she kneeled, her fingers tracing the letters etched into cold stone. "Marianne Phoenix," it read, a simple declaration of existence and its end. Here, amidst the departed, Carly found a rare kinship with the past, each visit a silent conversation with the mother who had left too soon, shaping the woman Carly had become.

"Hey, Mom," she murmured, a ritualistic greeting that bridged life and death. Carly didn't speak of triumphs or tribulations; instead, she shared the quiet of her soul, letting the peace of the place seep into her bones. It was here she could unmask herself, free from the guise of indomitable strength that her job demanded.

Yet amid the tranquility, a disturbance brushed the periphery of her senses—an intrusion that prickled at the back of her neck. Carly turned, her gaze cutting through the dimming light to land upon a figure standing a respectful distance away. Justin, her younger brother, the boy she herself had raised to a man, watched her with an expression that mirrored the complexity of the graveyard itself: sorrow interwoven with remembrance, love tinged with regret.

"Didn't expect to see you here," Carly said, rising to her feet and wiping dirt from her knees. Her voice was steady, but the surprise echoed silently within her. Their encounters were often calculated, rarely spontaneous, the remnants of a fractured bond.

"I come by some days," Justin replied, his hands buried deep in the pockets of his jacket. The wind toyed with his hair, stirring the dark locks in a dance of its own making.

She nodded, watching him edge closer, his movements hesitant, as if unsure of the welcome he might receive. Carly felt the old tug of familial ties, the push and pull that came with sharing a bloodline and history—a history marked by loss and the divergent paths they'd walked since.

"Seems we had the same idea," she said, the corner of her mouth lifting in a half-smile not quite reaching her eyes.

"Seems so," he agreed, stopping just shy of her side. Together, they stood in silent communion before the grave, the air between them charged with words unsaid, feelings unexpressed.

The cemetery was a sea of endings and echoes, and as Carly cast a sidelong glance at her brother, she wondered if among these markers of finality there might be room for new beginnings.

"Why are you here, Carly?" Justin asked, his face now etched with simmering resentment as if buried memories had just come to the fore.

"I wish I could tell you it was to find you, Justin," she said. "But that would be a lie."

"Then why? Just passing through?"

"No," Carly explained. "I've been given a job in Chicago. So, I could… I could be here for a while… If you want me to. I thought we could…"

"We could what?" Justin said. "Play happy families?"

"If you'll just let me explain…"

Justin turned his back and started walking away.

"Justin! She wouldn't have wanted us to fight like this!" Carly cried out. "I just want to make things right!"

Rain began to fall, covering the graveyard in a spray of watery mist. Justin turned around.

"She's dead, Sis," Justin said. "There's no making that right. But hell… You're a big-shot FBI agent now. You *know* what you should be doing."

"What?" Carly asked, her eyes red with rain and tears.

"Finding out who killed our mother, Carly," Justin said. "She was murdered. And I think you already know that deep down."

"Please… Justin… If we could only…"

"Leave me alone," Justin said. "It was better without you here."

Justin turned and walked between the gravestones until he vanished from sight. And Carly was left knowing, in her heart of hearts, that he was right.

It was time to find out who or what killed her mother.

NOW AVAILABLE!

COLD BLOODED
(A Carly Phoenix FBI Suspense Thriller—Book 2)

When a killer leaves cryptic poem stanzas at his crime scenes, FBI Agent Carly Phoenix finds herself in a deadly literary puzzle. Can she decode the lethal language to catch a killer from the past?

COLD BLOODED (A Carly Phoenix FBI Suspense Thriller—Book 2) is the second novel in a new series by mystery and suspense author Taylor Stark. The series begins with COLD JUSTICE (Book 1).

The Carly Phoenix series is an intense and riveting thriller featuring a complex and troubled female protagonist. Brimming with suspense, unexpected turns, and a pulse-pounding tempo, this series ensures an enthralling experience that's bound to keep you turning pages late into the night. Fans of Karin Slaughter, Teresa Driscoll, and Lisa Regan are sure to fall in love.

Future books in the series are also available!

Taylor Stark

Taylor Stark is author of the MARY CAGE mystery series, comprising five books (and counting); of the CARLY PHOENIX mystery series, comprising five books (and counting); and of the new SIENNA DUSK mystery series, comprising five books (and counting).

An avid reader and lifelong fan of the mystery and thriller genres, Taylor loves to hear from you, so please feel free to visit taylorstarkauthor.com to learn more and stay in touch.

BOOKS BY TAYLOR STARK

MARY CAGE SUSPENSE THRILLER
FAR FROM HERE (Book #1)
FAR FROM HOPE (Book #2)
FAR FROM SAFE (Book #3)
FAR FROM SIGHT (Book #4)
FAR FROM REACH (Book #5)

CARLY PHOENIX SUSPENSE THRILLER
COLD JUSTICE (Book #1)
COLD BLOODED (Book #2)
COLD TRUTH (Book #3)
COLD PURSUIT (Book #4)
COLD VENGEANCE (Book #5)

SIENNA DUSK SUSPENSE THRILLER
BENEATH THE FROST (Book #1)
BENEATH THE SURFACE (Book #2)
BENEATH THE LIES (Book #3)
BENEATH THE SILENCE (Book #4)
BENEATH THE WHISPERS (Book #5)

Made in the USA
Monee, IL
18 July 2024

61897718R00095